The Sunset Of Love

Joel Solomon Tekenate

Love Is Still In Your Heart

In the morning
The sun rises
Love sprouts and blossoms

Her leaves fade and dry out
In the evening
At sun set

The night comes
And the grass returns to source with decay
Then everything becomes a tale

Life is just for the name
Love is just a game
When everybody wants to play

To those who have loved
And to those who no longer love
Love is still in your heart

To those who fear to love
And to those who still want to love
Love is still in your heart

To those who still love
And to those who may never love
Love is still in your heart

ACKNOWLEDGEMENTS

My sincere heartfelt gratitude to God Almighty who gives gifts and talents unto men; for it is not of him that wills, nor of him that runs but of God who shows mercy.

Special thanks to all the members of my family: my Dee, my dad, my younger brothers and sisters for their contributions, ceaseless words of encouragement, inspiration, motivation and support.

Special thanks to all my friends and relatives for their contributions, ceaseless words of encouragement, inspiration, motivation and support.

Finally, special thanks to all who inspired, contributed and helped in one way or the other to the success of the work.

You made this happen.

Thanks a million.

Joel Solomon Tekenate

Chapter 1

Ebitobho was one of those few privileged young men that had never experienced any heartbreak. Actually, he was one of the young men doing the dirty job of breaking the heart of every innocent young woman that crossed their path. He just walked into any naive heart, took a strong hold of that fragile glass which they call the heart, smashed it on the ground, crushed it to pieces with his heels and just moved on with his beautiful carefree life without taking a second look at what he had done.

He did the appalling job without any atom of remorse, sense of care or apology. Surprisingly, the more he did the dirty job, the more new ones fall for him. Sometimes, it seems like Nature was even rewarding him with new prey whenever he successfully accomplished any task. When he dropped the old ones that he had devoured, more innocent ones flock around him and made themselves available for destruction. Soon they also become victims of his merciless claws and paws.

When you look at him, you will agree that Nature had indeed endowed him for the job. He was very handsome, tall and dark in complexion. He was smart, intelligent, humorous and fun to be with. He was sociable and friendly. You can hardly spend few minutes with him and would not long to spend more time with him. He knew how to engage people in long conversations and was so good at amusing his audience with his several funny stories and jokes. Being an undergraduate that was studying English and Literary Studies at the prestigious University of Port Harcourt, the dangerous player was fully fortified and equipped with all the necessary language arsenal and wooing prowess to lure his prey to the slaughter. He was also working in a reputable oil company and was earning some good salary, and that fortified him financially for all his romantic escapades.

Ebitobho was one of those wild young men who could hardly stick to one woman for more than a month. Whenever any prey visits his slaughter room, he loses his interest. Without any warning, he will break up and start seeking for another naïve prey. Some of his friends called him the predator who only devours and feasts on fresh prey. Sometimes, he boldly declared to his friends that he was on a secret assignment to beat the Guinness Record of King Solomon of Old, before he would tie the knot and settle down with the doomed love of his life. Looking at him, you will agree that he meant his words.

While Ebitobho was having so much fun doing his awful thing, his bosom friend, Ifiyemi, was having a different experience. Ifiyemi was on the receiving side. He had already received five hot whiplashes of heartbreak and had not even recovered from the last experience.

Ebitobho and Ifiyemi became bosom friends when they discovered that they were from the same ethnicity. Although, they belonged to two different clans, however, their villages were very close.

Some people covered the distance between their villages within thirty minutes' walk.

The bosom friends actually came to know each other in the Garden City. Their apartments were almost directly opposite each other. Thus, whenever they were free, they usually spent quality time together drinking and chatting.

"This weather is just too cold for me this evening," Ifiyemi complained.

"You know what to do when the weather is too cold for you. Don't seek for counsel tactically when you already know what to do," Ebitobho replied.

The bosom friends had just seen off one of Ebitobho's new girlfriends to the gate of the Marine Estate, where they were residing at the moment. They were walking gradually, side-by-side, towards their residence in the estate.

Ifiyemi stopped abruptly. Ebitobho noticed it and he also stopped. He looked at his friend and wondered what had prompted him to stop suddenly. Just then, Ifiyemi spoke out.

"Oh mehn! How are you doing it? Ifiyemi asked.

"I don't understand your question, my friend. What do you really mean?" Ebitobho asked.

"Mehn, girls don suffer for your hand oh. I just dey wonder why dem just dey flock around you like bees all the time. How you dey take do am?" Ifiyemi asked and Ebitobho began to laugh.

"I no dey do anything special my friend. However, my hands are always open. Whenever they walk in; I embrace them and grab the opportunity sharp-sharp. You know, man must wack nah. However, I

don't take anything serious after every experience. If the monkey enjoy the banana well-well, e go surely come back for more. However, when I don't want it again, I plainly tell the person and we go our separate ways. Shikinah! That is the way I do my thing," Ebitobho said, smiling.

"Chai! Guy, you bad!" Ifiyemi responded.

"No be small thing," Ebitobho said, laughing. "You see, it is just a game. When you have scored the desired number of goals; you just have to move on."

"Hmm! See levels! When will I develop the kind of heart you have?"

"I don't have a different heart, my friend."

"You can tell that story to the wind, my dear."

"Ha ha ha! Let me tell you something. There is no smoke without fire. When you see a very heartless man, don't judge him hastily. Sometimes, that same person might have been a very good person in the past," Ebitobho said.

"Are you admitting that you are bad?"

"That is not what I am saying," Ebitobho replied laughing.

"But that is what you said."

"English is not my mother tongue, my friend."

"Look at who is talking! *Abeg, leave that thing jareh.* Em... Ehen... You talked about experience. Are you saying you have also experienced a heartbreak in the past?" Ifiyemi asked.

"Nope! Never! I have not and will never experience it."

"Why do you think so?"

"Because I learn from the experiences of other people."

"Experiences of other people!"

"Yeah."

"Tell me about it."

"I have always learned from people like you."

"You don start? Leave that thing joor! You didn't learn anything from me. You have always been like this since I knew you. You have not changed one bit," Ifiyemi said.

"Well, I have not changed because I have been learning from your own experiences," Ebitobho responded.

"Please, tell me the things you have been learning from my experiences."

"I don't think you will learn anything. If you will, your personal painful experiences should have taught you a lot. If your own bitter experiences did not change you, then, another person's experience will just be a mare tale. You have had several ugly experiences of heartbreak yet you have decided to remain naïve. You don't want to grow up. So just remain there and enjoy your lot."

"I might just learn the things you want me to learn today if you can just talk about it. Even if I don't change immediately; I could learn something that could change me in the future. Leave the matter of change and let me just enjoy the gist," Ifiyemi said.

"Story that touches the heart! Please, leave me alone! You will not learn anything."

"Stop this shakara and give me the gist, my friend!" Ifiyemi yelled.

"See person! Your shout no go fit drive fly wey stand on top of cold eba. Soon you go dey cry for one small girl. Abeg, commot for here!" Ebitobho replied, laughing. "

"You no wan talk about it?"

"You know what to do. You have to bribe me, else I will not tell you anything. When you pay for my services, you will value it."

"Ha ha ha! Services! Hmm... So what do you want?"

"You know that I don't ask for something big. Take me to the usual place, The Meeting Point Bar, and throw three bottles of beer at me, and I will open my mouth wide like the hippopotamus and give you the gist of your life."

"Rubbish! You no dey shame!"

"Wetin wan make me shame nah?"

"You wan take bribe from your very own best friend."

"That is no longer a breaking news. My friend has done it to me before. I have also done it to him before. We have done it to each other several times. We enjoy doing it to each other all the time."

"But bros, that doesn't make it right."

"Make una see wetin my guy suppose preach as Sunday Sermon oh! Haba! You don forget say today na Friday? Wetin you go preach on Sunday morning nah? Abeg, go park your face for dirty."

"You no get respect for your elders again, abi? Make una see dis small boy oh! You too, go park your face for dirty!"

"You can keep your money, my friend; and let me keep my gist. After all, you are the one who wants to hear the gist. In fact, I am not even in the mode of giving you any gist. That is why I wanted the three bottles of beer to *ginger my swagger* so that I can give you the gist of your life *but you wan preach moral wey you no get. Who give you moral nah? You wan make I wash your dirty clothes for outside? You wey rotten pass rotten egg! Abegi! Make I hear something."*

"Insult me as you like. When you finish I will go and give you beer. *Since na only beer your head dey think about, no worry, you go drink am today.* My problem is that somebody's precious child will soon turn into a drunkard."

"I am already one and you are also one. The other day you vomited on your bed after drinking palm wine, stout and hot drink. I don't have such a horrible record," Ebitobho said.

"Look at you! Yours is even worse. You slept off in front of the bottles of beer that you have guzzled into your stomach right at the bar, and right before the eyes of the public. I don't have such a shameful record," Ifiyemi said, and both of them laughed.

"My brother, that experience was the ugly peak of my drinking career. Imagine the madness and the nonsense! But I won't blame myself *sha!* I tried. You know, I went for the all-night club experience. When I returned, we all went for that our neighbour's wedding ceremony. After the wedding ceremony, we went straight to the bar for another drinking experience when the leftover of the previous night was still working in my system. You were just fortunate that you did not follow us to the club; else, your own story would have been more pathetic. In fact, your case would have been *sorry,*" Ebitobho said they laughed.

Chapter 2

The weekend drinking extravaganza had already started at The Meeting Point Bar when they arrived. There were several people at the bar and almost all the tables were already occupied with people. The bar was always crowded at weekends. The usual crowd was already gathering.

The bar was located within the Marine Estate, which was divided into two parts by a tarred road. The bar was located at the end of the tarred road. It had a cemented open space beside the sea, which was a wide tributary that flowed into the Atlantic Ocean. A big umbrella tree stood gallantly and stretched its branches over the cemented open space.

Cold breeze from the sea blew continually towards the bar to massage the body of those who came to patronize there. During the day, when the sun was hot, people stayed under the umbrella tree, which was beside the bar. However, in the evenings, they spread their tables beyond the branches of the umbrella tree.

The bar was a great site to view the sea. It was also a nice place to cool off at every time of the day due to the cold sea breeze that blew towards the bar always.

The two friends took a table and sat down opposite each other. It was the last available table. There were nine tables at the bar at the moment. Each of the nine tables had four chairs. Even though all the nine tables were already occupied, some of the chairs were still vacant. More tables and chairs were usually arranged when more people arrive.

Immediately they settled down, Ifiyemi called the waiter and ordered for two bottles of stout, the favourite brand of beer for the two friends. They only took something different when they don't have any other option. All the waiters at this bar knew their favourite brand of beer. Thus, sometimes, the waiters brought it for them before they could even open their mouths to make orders.

"I want to chew something. You had better order for fried snails, my friend," Ebitobho said.

"Hmm! All this one na because you want tell me one yeye story abi? Oyioburu na turn by turn oh! Take am easy, my friend. The cane wey you take flog the back of another person may someday fall on your own back without mercy. Your own day might just be at the corner," Ifiyemi said.

"Well, I am only learning from you. You have done this to me several times happily. This is my opportunity and I will utilize it to the full," Ebitobho responded, laughing.

"No problem! Today is your day. Demand for anything and I will give it to you willingly," Ifiyemi said.

Ifiyemi ordered for two plates of fried sails when the drinks arrived. The waiter opened the drinks and left the two friends to enjoy themselves. The plates of snails also arrived on their table as Ebitobho and Ifiyemi filled their glasses and took their first sip.

"Hmm! This beer is the original."

"Wetin dey sweet you for body? Will you just shut up your mouth and drink your beer? When last did you drink an imitation at this bar? Have you ever taken any beer that was an imitation? *Be like say* this *one glass don dey make you high?"*

"Wetin concern you? Na your mouth I dey take drink or talk? Your body don dey pepper you because I dey chop your money, abi? Oya, go hug transformer nah. Abeg, shift!"

"Commot there! How much you go fit chop? You go fit drink? How many bottles you go fit drink nah? You don drink one crate of beer before? You wan die? Abeggi! Make I hear something," Ifiyemi said.

"If you like make your body dey pepper you die; I no dey look your face. As you dey see me so; I just dey enjoy myself."

"Enjoy yourself my friend! *Nothing do you."*

"Thank you. Hmm... I am feeling so good that I am making some people spend their hard earned money. Wow! What a privilege!" Ebitobho said, laughing.

"It's your day. Enjoy yourself, my friend," Ifiyemi replied, also laughing.

"Thank you very much. Em... Ok... Now that you have fulfilled one third of my demands, let me give you the gist that you have paid for," Ebitobho said, still laughing.

"Go ahead, my friend. But please, don't forget; *oyioburu na turn by turn.*"

"Shut up, my friend! You no get respect? If I hear another pim from you; I will just pocket my gist, drink your beer, chop your snail and waka go my house. Nothing go happen!"

"I'm sorry, Sah!" Ifiyemi said and both of them laughed.

"Here is my story," Ebitobho began after taking another sip of beer from his glass after their laughter. "I once had a neighbour. He was a very good friend but more like a big brother. He was far older than I. The young man was a captain and he was making some good money. I greatly benefitted from him when I had no job. In those days, no one in our compound could say that he or she did not receive a gift from this generous young man. This young captain helped everyone who went to him for help. Apart from that, every Christmas celebration, specifically on the 24th night, this young man will kill a big sheep and will use the whole meat for pepper soup. He will invite the whole compound, and some of his friends and well-wishers to eat and drink with him. My friend, you will eat meat until your stomach will be filled. If you don't drink wisely; *your body go tell you. My brother, na so. Every year, na so we dey flex with this guy.* Then, this guy ran into one beautiful lady. My brother, that babe was indeed very beautiful. She was very tall, about six feet, and quite huge: perfect height and size. She was one of those rare girls that were heavily endowed front and back. She was fair in complexion, and her fair skin was spotless. When you look at her, her jewelries will speak out and tell you that she has taste for gold. Her clothes will tell you her class. You can't see her and not turn to admire her and praise the One Who had created her. This young captain fell in love with this lady. He loved her so much. In fact, he was crazy about her. Soon, he married her and began to spoil her with everything that money can buy. Even though they never had any child, nevertheless, the young man still loved her and showered her with love. Every year, he bought a new car to celebrate her birthday," Ebitobho paused, took another sip of his beer and continued.

"Nevertheless, I don't know why this young woman was not faithful to him. Whenever the young man travelled out of town for of his job, she will start having affairs with other men who can't even stand before this young man in wealth and physical looks. Sometimes, she even brought them into their matrimonial home. You may be wondering how I knew some of these things? Well, I was her watchdog. The young captain heard about her secret affairs and he paid me to monitor her. He paid me some good money to do the job for him and I did it and I paid other guys and we monitored her when he was not around. We monitored her and discovered that she had four other boyfriends. I was heartbroken when I found out about her unfaithfulness. I was so hurt. It was as though I was the one that was marrying her. When her husband was around, she acted as though she could not kill a fly. Whenever, I remember that captain's heartbreaking experience; I classify every woman in the same category," Ebitobho said.

"There are some good and faithful women out there, my friend."

"Please, keep your comments to yourself. What do you know about women?" Ebitobho asked.

"I have seen some good women."

"Ha ha ha! You have been deceived by their pretense."

"I am not deceived. I know what I am talking about. I know..."

"What do you know?" Ebitobho interrupted sharply. "What do you want to say about women? Your own experiences have not proved me wrong! In fact, they have only helped to strengthen my old beliefs. So what do you want to say? Please, keep all your beautiful comments until you run into one of those good and faithful women, then you can call me and defend them. Else, don't sit in front of me to say anything good about women."

"Well... Em... It's ok. You can continue with your story. Let's leave that argument for the right time," Ifiyemi said.

"Good," Ebitobho responded, took another sip and continued. "Mehn, this captain was rich and he spent the money on her recklessly. This guy bought a house close to our compound. He demolished the building and erected a new one in less than six months. It was the most beautiful house along our street for several years. If you enter that house you will know what taste looks like. In fact, you will know that taste has a voice. My brother, in all these luxury, this woman could not remain faithful to her husband. To cut the long story; I informed him and we planned and caught her right in their matrimonial home with another man. The young captain was so angry that he shut both of them and killed them right on their matrimonial bed. He took himself to the police station and reported the incident. The police came with a van and an ambulance, and took the two lifeless bodies to the mortuary before arresting him. The matter was immediately charged to court and he was charged with manslaughter and was sentenced to several years imprisonment.

Since from that ugly experience; I have not taken any woman seriously," Ebitobho concluded.

"Hmm! That is a very sad story, nevertheless, I still think, there are some good women out there. If there are bad women, there should be good women too," Ifiyemi said.

"You want to preach to me about women! How many good ones have you experienced in your life? Why did you choose to stick to sex workers instead of getting one of those descent good girls out there? Do you want me to insult you in the bid of challenging your opinions before you will keep quiet?"

"Please, don't start. I am not ready for it today," Ifiyemi said laughing.

"Fine, then you had better not make me go there," Ebitobho said, laughing also.

They remained silent for a while as they took their drinks and ate the snails.

"Thanks for the gist," Ifiyemi said, breaking the silence again.

"You are welcome. Now you have an idea about the pathetic story behind my madness," Ebitobho said.

"Yes I do, but I earnestly pray that you will meet a very good woman that will change your negative perception about women someday," Ifiyemi said.

"Amen oh!" Ebitobho echoed in a very funny way and both of them laughed.

The both friends continued to enjoy their drinks and snails. At this time, each of them was on the second bottle of beer and the second plate of fried snails. They talked about other things and laughed as they took their beer and ate their snails. When each of them was about to finish the third bottle of beer and the third plate of fried snails, Ebitobho called the attention of his friend.

"Ifiyemi!"

"Yes. I am here."

"I will be travelling to the village tomorrow. I want to go and see my parents. I will come back on Sunday."

"Chai! I will miss you so much."

"Hey! When did that 'I will miss you so much' thing start? Now, I know that beer is talking through you, Mr. Drunkard!"

"Na you be Mr. Drunkard. No be you push me come here?"

"I no push you oh! Na you carry your two legs waka come here! I know what you will be missing. When I return on Sunday, I will bring you here and pay for the hospitality you have shown today. When I bring you here on Sunday, whenever I drink one bottle, you can drink seven bottles of beer to make up for the Saturday evening that I will not be around. By the time, I take my third bottle; you should have taken twenty one bottles of beer. I am sure that will be very good for your little brain," Ebitobho said.

"I am not a drunkard. I drink responsibly," Ifiyemi replied.

"I know. You don't have to tell me. I have seen people like you who drink responsibly but got drunk and even vomited on their own beds in this very city. When I look at your face, I can see the face of a responsible drunkard. Rubbish!"

"I have also seen people like you, who drink responsibly but got so drunk that they bowed their heads on the table and slept right in front of the empty bottles of beer at the bar. When I look at your face, I can also see the face of a responsible drunkard. Rubbish!" Ifiyemi retorted and they laughed.

The bosom friends talked and laughed as whey finished their third bottles of beer and their third plates of snails. Ifiyemi paid the bills and they walked home to have their night rest.

Chapter 3

Ebitobho dropped from the bus which had carried him from Yenagoa to Abali Motor Park as the sun continued its skating journey into the dark western horizon. He was returning to the city from the village. He had gone to the village to visit his aged parents. He usually went to the village to visit them at the end of every month when he had received his salary. He had actually gone to the village to give some money to his aged parents.

He walked out of the gate of the motor park and joined a bus to Lagos Bus Stop. When he dropped from the bus along Aggrey Road, some motorcycle riders that were waiting to carry passengers to their destinations quickly rode towards him and stopped in front of him. They throttled their engines noisily in front of him one after the other.

Motorcycle riders in Port Harcourt City usually did this whenever they locate someone that may require their services. After listening to the sounds of the motorcycle engines as the motorcycle riders throttled them nosily at different times before him; he chose the newest one, whose engine seemed to give the best sound than the others. He climbed the motorcycle and left the bus-stop. However, just as they were riding towards Harbour Road, Ebitobho saw Juliet walking towards Lagos Bus-Stop.

Ebitobho and Juliet used to live in the same compound years ago. They were very close neighbours when they lived in a face-me-I-face-you twelve bed-sitters compound at Nanka Street. At that time, Ebitobho was living with his uncle, Wari, while Juliet was living with her parents.

Ebitobho and Juliet also had some affection for each other but they had never had the opportunity to express it as Uncle Wari and Juliet's parents kept vigilant eyes on them. Ebitobho finally left his uncle's house as he secured his own apartment at Harbour Road when he started working in a multinational oil company. Juliet and her parents also packed to Rumuola few months after Ebitobho had packed from the compound. Since then, they had not seen each other. They only heard about each other from friends and neighbours; for those were the days that only some few privileged elites used NITEL telephones in their houses in the city of Port Harcourt.

"Julie!" Ebitobho shouted.

Juliet turned quickly and saw him passing by on the motorcycle.

"Ebi!" she also shouted and beckoned on him to stop.

Suddenly the motorcyclist reversed and came towards her and stopped beside her. Immediately Ebitobho dropped from the motorcycle, Juliet jumped and clung onto him like a wild cat, her hands strongly wrapped around his neck and her legs wrapped around his waist.

"Hey!" Ebitobho exclaimed as he staggered backwards carrying her in his arms. "What was that?" he asked.

"I call it a public show of excitement. Just to tell you how much I missed you."

"Ha ha ha! You are very fortunate that I swallowed enough *eba* in the village this morning before coming to the city, else, we would have crashed landed on the ground like a mud-house blown down by a strong wind."

"That would have just been perfect for me to carry out the old plan I have been nursing for years."

"What is that old plan you have been nursing for years?"

"When I had remained on top of you and happily rocked you like a wild horse, you would have known without being told what I have been nursing for years."

"What! What did you say?"

"You heard me. Stop pretending."

"Hmm! See groove! Sorry, your evil desire was cut short."

"That is not an evil desire. It is just a romantic desire," Juliet corrected.

"Oh, I see! By their words, ye shall know them."

"What is the meaning of that? Stop quoting the Scriptures upside down, Mr. Pastor. Do you want to invite the wrath of the Almighty to descend on you like a wild fire? Remember, our God is a consuming fire," she retorted.

"Wow! I never knew you are an Evangelist." Ebitobho said.

"I am learning from you, Pastor," she said and they laughed.

Their strange emotional embrace was already attracting the ever wandering curious eyes of passers-by as they remained locked up in each other's arms. Ebitobho saw the motorcyclist – who had at this time, turned off the engine of the motorcycle – shaking his head with smiles. Ebitobho winked at him with a smile and the man shook his head again and continued to smile.

"Wow! Long time no see!" Ebitobho said as they finally disengaged with smiles, when they could no longer withstand the sharp piercing eyes that were feasting on them.

"You can say that again," Juliet said, still smiling.

Ebitobho's eyes slowly travelled from her beautifully braided hair which gave a beautiful fitting to her small skull and her well powdered smooth and round face. Then, to her molded moderate mountains that were held captive in a tight blue blouse, then to her flat stomach and her wide hips and finally to her straight and spotless fair complexioned legs, being advertised accidentally by her short, black skirt which rested above her knees. He couldn't help licking his lips as his eyes explored the alluring and irresistible beauty that was standing before him.

"Mmm mmm!" Juliet cleared her throat deliberately as she noticed the movement of his eyes from her head to her toes. "I hope someone will not end up tearing my clothes apart with the sharp piercing blades of his eyes and expose my hidden treasures to every eye on this Port Harcourt road?" she teased.

"You got me red handed," Ebitobho said, laughing and she also joined him in the laughter. "I am very sorry to have torn your clothes apart with my eyes, which are indeed sharper than razor blades. In fact, I have already seen everything that you are hiding under those clothes. Trust me; I am so impressed with what my eyes saw. I must confess that you are so endowed, your Royal Majesty."

“What! That is a criminal act, capable of reducing the high value of my bride pride. You had better control your lustful eyes. Don’t you dare allow it to travel beyond boundary or else I will tell my parents and your parents about this unpardonable and abominable crime you have committed against the pride of my womanhood,” Juliet replied with a serious look on her face and started laughing again.

“I don’t mind if you can just do it at once. I think, that will serve as the first stage of the introduction to our marriage rites, which my people usually call the ‘Knocking of Door.’ I am ready to face the glorious penalty of my honourable crime that will take me into the safe prison of your heart. That has been my secret desire all these years.”

“All these years?”

“Oh yeah! Have you forgotten how I have always longed to have you as mine?”

“Hmm! I see.”

“Don’t blame me? The eye likes good things. When it sees a good thing, it will not require a town crier to announce it. Your presence has just awakened my eyes from its slumber and the blinding scale of darkness that covered them has just been swept off by the wild wind of admiration. I had no choice than to allow my eyes feast on your beauty and become satisfied by the intoxicating sight of the most adorable icon of beauty that could satisfy any holy or unholy eye. My dear, indeed you are an epitome of beauty. Your beauty will continue to satisfy the heart of any privileged man that could have you as his own.”

“Grammar! I can bet with my cup of tea that you would have beaten William Shakespeare in a literary contest if you had the opportunity to compete with him," Juliet said, smiling and Ebitobho laughed.

"Did you say your cup of tea?"

"Yes. Em… Do you want me to use my plate of rice?"

"You are so naughty."

"I learnt it from you?"

"You are not serious," Ebitobho replied as both of them continued to laugh. "But seriously, you are so beautiful. I can't help but lust after you so shamelessly and publicly."

"Please, stop flattering me."

"I am not flattering you. I would be lying, if I had said anything different," Ebitobho said smiling. "Well, at this point, I will agree with the elders that say even though the eyes could see everything in front, it has not been able to see the beauty of the face that is in front."

"Ha ha ha! What kind of parable is that?"

"Those who eat with the elders usually speak the language of the elders. Those who eat with children also learn to speak the language of children."

"Please, leave all these bizarre proverbs of yours? You will never change; always using words and expressions that are bigger than your small coconut head," she replied smiling.

Juliet's eyes also crawled from his small lips to his round dark face, then from his thick curly hair to his neatly lined mustache and goatee, then down to his round and full neck, which rested on his broad chest, and finally to his flat stomach that announced his masculine and athletic physique.

"Hey! You look so well-fed. I have looked at you so closely and I am wondering who has been feeding you so well with her nutritious breast milk?" she teased with a wink, still smiling.

"Sorry… Nutritious what?"

"You heard me."

"I don't know what you are talking about," Ebitobho responded and started laughing.

"Indeed! Pretenders do the worst," Juliet replied.

"Meaning?" Ebitobho asked.

"That's pretense of the highest degree and I can see it all over your face. I know that people like you can't live without it. They live on it daily like sucklings. If you ever deny them, they will cry shamelessly like hungry babies and right before your very eyes."

"That is a preposterous and outlandish assertion, capable of demeaning and relegating my humble and honourable personality to a state of nihility. Such an act of rubbishing the gargantuan grandeur of my noble reputation and soiling it with such a nauseating debauchery of shame is punishable in the Nigerian Court of Justice," Ebitobho said with a very serious look on his face that could frighten a fearful child.

"Exactly!" Juliet replied, laughing. "But I can see it written all over your face. Your look is betraying you. Even your eyes are betraying you. It is so glaring that even the blind can attest to my claims. *Chai!* What a pity!"

"That is an observation projected solely for the destruction and annihilation of my righteous reputation. Please, kindly desist from such felony and delinquency. I am a very humble bachelor, who always cooks for himself. Moreover, grey haired people like me don't live on 'bee' milk."

"Wow! 'Bee' milk! I have not heard that before. I never knew you have already given it such a beautiful baptisimal name," she said and they laughed.

"That is not true. The word was just too sacred for me to pronounce."

"Sacred indeed! Wait a minute! Did I hear you say grey haired people like you don't live on 'bee' milk?"

"Exactly! Come closer and take a very good and careful look at the hairs on my head and you will also attest to the strands of white hairs on my head."

"If they are there as you have claimed, I don't have to take a very good and careful look to see them."

"Yes, I know, but I was just trying to help when I noticed that you cannot see them from afar. As a very good friend who always wants the best for you; I am recommending one of those big binocular, medicated and magnifying glasses. It will help you see very well, my dear. You can even see the future."

"I am sure you also want to see the future. So how many have you bought for yourself?"

"But I have observed that you need them."

"Dear, my eyes can see far better than the eyes of the eagle but let's leave that argument for now. You are craftily changing our subject of discussion."

"What is our subject of discussion?"

"Don't worry! You will soon remember. I know that you will not accept that men like you live on 'bee' milk. A day will come and you will agree with me that 'grey haired people like you' still request for 'bee' milk and sometimes they even beg for it more than sucklings. Pray that the day you will ask for it, I should not be around. If I am there, you will kneel down and beg for it with seven drums of tears and seven buckets of sweat before you will get a taste of it," Juliet said with such determination in her voice and both of them laughed again.

"Bros, na wetin be this nah?" the motorcyclist suddenly interrupted angrily. *"Abeg, make una come give me my money before una continue with this una long talk wey no dey gree end. Haba!"*

"Ewoh! Abeg, sorry. No vex! No blame us; we never see each other for several years."

"That one no concern me nah. Abeg, make una settle me, make I commot for here. Make una no dey waste my time. Time na money," the man said.

"We no forget you oh. We were just carried away," Ebitobho responded, smiling.

"This one pass carried away nah. From wetin I dey see, I know say una no fit hold una self again. Oya, make una come enter okada. Make una come go house quick-quick go finish the rest before the fire quench," the man teased and Ebitobho and Juliet laughed.

"Bros, you wan spoil me o!" Juliet said as they continued to laugh heartily.

"Ehn! Spoil you? Abi dem dey spoil something wey don already spoil kpata-kpata? Na me teach you how to climb man for road? All the press-press wey you dey take your body dey press-press am, na me

teach you? All the drama wey you dey act for me for here, na me teach you?" the man asked with an intonation that aroused more laughter.

He spoke very slowly with a coarse tone, and in a manner that one would think that the words were too heavy for his tongue. He pronounced them gradually and slowly, releasing them like heavy loads, which fell on their ears with great reverberation, stirring up laughter.

"Bros, you are correct," Ebitobho said. "Julie, the man has just said what I wanted to say all this while. You have to follow me to the house. I want you to follow me and find out where I have been hiding all these years so that..."

"Una go finish the good work wey una don start for road," the motorcyclist interrupted and completed the sentence for him, arousing another round of laughter for Ebitobho and Juliet while the man remained as though he had not said anything funny.

"That wouldn't be necessary," Juliet said after the round of laughter.

"Abeg, leave oyibo and stop your initial gara-gara. Abi na becoz I advise una say make una go finish the good work for house? If I no talk like that, you for no follow am go finish am? I know say you wan go finish the thing for house. I don see am for your eyes. Abeg, come join okada make I carry una go the place wey una go finish the good work wey una don happily start for dis main road," the man said, igniting the engine of the motorcycle at the same time and throttling it noisily.

Ebitobho and Juliet looked at each other speechlessly and suddenly walked towards the man and climbed the motorcycle as if they were being remote-controlled by the man's speech.

"I am sure you hired this man to speak on your behalf," Juliet said as the motorcycle began to move.

"Yes, I did," Ebitobho said.

"How much did he pay you, *Oga*?" Juliet asked the man.

"Seventeen bottles of *kaikai,"* the man said and Ebitobho and Juliet exploded into another raucous laughter but the man remained silent. He didn't even give out a smile let alone laughing with them. They continued to laugh and tears began to flow down from the sides of Juliet's eyes. She had never expected such an answer from the man.

"You go kill me with laughter before we get to our destination," Juliet said still laughing.

"Where you wan die go? If you try am, trust me, the magic fingers of your boyfriend knows how to touch you and wake you up from the dead," the man responded making Juliet to choke with more laughter.

"Which kin man be dis wey you bring come to carry me today?" Juliet asked Ebitobho as she wiped the tears flowing down her cheeks.

"It has been appointed before the foundation of the world for us to meet today so that you could follow me to my house."

"And after that?" Juliet asked.

"Engagement and marriage ceremony," responded Ebitobho.

"Hmm... See groove! I dey fear this kin divine arrangement wey you dey talk about oh. I hope say you no be one of those prophets of doom! I hope say this divine arrangement will last forever," Juliet said.

"You don't have to worry about that. Time will surely answer all your questions."

The motorcyclist suddenly stopped as he arrived at the bus-stop Ebitobho had earlier told him. Both of them dropped and Ebitobho handed some money to the man.

"Please keep the change," Ebitobho said. "You have done noble for compelling this beautiful queen to follow me to my house. I don't know if she would have followed me, if you were not there to assist. Thank you for all the assistance."

"Don't make his head swell like a big balloon. I came with you because I secretly really wanted to know where you are staying," Juliet said.

"Wow! I never knew that. Thank you for that true confession," Ebitobho responded with smiling.

"Bros, today na today. Today na your day. Carry go! The sweet banana wey monkey dey find for your house, make you go give am plenty. If this flat belle wey I dey see no grow big; then you be very stingy, selfish and greedy man. But I no see selfishness and greed for your face. Abeg, go give am plenty banana make the thing full her flat belle. Go take am sharp-sharp before she change her mind oh. Opportunity comes but ones," the man said, smiling for the first time, throttled his engine noisily and rode off.

Ebitobho and Juliet looked at each other and laughed again. Ebitobho turned and kept on looking at the man until he gradually disappeared from his view.

Chapter 4

Ebitobho greeted and waved at several neighbours and acquaintances as they walked towards his apartment. Noticing the stirring eyes in the neighbourhood, her presence gave him an air of importance as they walked side by side together towards his apartment.

"Brother, welcome," a little girl greeted and ran towards them.

She had walked out from one of the apartments of the building he was staying. Ebitobho lifted her shoulder high, threw her into the air three times and caught her. He played with her a bit as those in their apartments also came out and greeted them as they heard his voice. Finally, he dropped the little girl and gave her some money.

"Thank you, Brother," the girl said and happily ran back into the room she had earlier emerged.

The mother of the little girl soon came out, greeted and thanked him as he was still outside, trying to open his door. He responded, opened the door of the apartment and walked in. Juliet also followed him.

"This is where I have been hiding all these years," Ebitobho said as they walked into the room.

Her eyes quickly moved from the large bed to the two upholstery chairs; from the window air-conditioner to the double door refrigerator; from the beautiful curtain to the colour of the paint on the wall; and finally settled on the 21 inches television set that stood gallantly on a wooden stand that had shelves and a glass door which housed a VCD player, a video player and a radio set.

"You have a very beautiful place," Juliet said.

"Thank you, please sit down," Ebitobho said as he switched on the television and the air-conditioner then, closed the door and walked towards her.

"You hugged me on the road in such a way that made me shy. Now I want to hug you properly in my own way that will also make you shy," Ebitobho said walking towards her.

"I never knew you were shy. So I was actually torturing you right there! Serves you right," Juliet said, laughing.

"All the same, I enjoyed it. You have taught me never to be shy again," he said.

"Ha ha ha! You should have shown me a bit of it out there. I love such outside show of love. I want to scar your admirers and make them jealous. I don't usually show the same affection when we get to the house because it could lead to several things that one could have avoided," Juliet said.

"Naughty child... However, you are such an amazing person," Ebitobho said, laughing. "Come here," he said, as he pulled her gently and she stood up.

They hugged each other again but this time it ended in a passionate breath-taking kiss, their hands crawling slowly on each other's back like a millipede, setting each other's nerves on fire but Ebitobho suddenly disengaged.

"What am I doing? Have I lost my godly manners by this temptation? How could I treat my beauty Queen, the present Miss Universe with such a despicable act of disrespect? This kind of crime could send one to the peak of the mountain in few seconds. Please accept my sincere apology, your Royal Majesty. I am sorry for that sudden outburst of my emotions," Ebitobho said bowing down his head in a hypocritical courtesy and both of them began to laugh. "What can I offer my Queen?" Ebitobho asked as he left her and walked towards the refrigerator.

"A cold glass of that milky substance, stored in the freezer of your scrotal sac could quench the fire burning in my veins," she teased with a seductive smile, winking her eyes at him at the same time.

Ebitobho stopped abruptly, turned and looked at her with a look of disbelief. Then he smiled, shaking his head at the same time. "Sorry, I don't have the cold one but I can offer you the warm one. I have abundant stock."

"If it is cold, then, I will prefer a hot juicy kiss to wet my throat and quench the dehydrating thirst that I feel within my chest."

"You just had some."

"I guess it was not enough."

"I thought you needed something more. I have an abundant stock of that too and you can never exhaust it. Make sure, you don't ask for too much. Our elders say that the food that is too delicious for the tongue; usually makes the flat stomach of the lizard to rise like a mountain."

"Don't also forget that the one who cooks the delicious meal also expects someone to eat it, else it will become sour and useless," Juliet replied.

The two lovebirds walked into each other's arms again and were soon drowning in the deep ocean of thrilling sensations. Wild currents of sensations flowed through their entire being as they feasted on each other's lips. Cold thrilling sensations flowed through their immune systems and millions of goose bumps grew on their smooth skins like pimples and boils as their hands moved and crawled on each other's soft skin. Then suddenly, there was a gentle knock at the door.

"Kpo! Kpo!"

"Oh no! Who is this person that has been sent to disrupt this magic flow?" Ebitobho said to himself as they disengaged quickly. "Yes! Come in," he said breathlessly as they struggled in vain to straighten their rumpled clothes and sat down abruptly on the upholsteries as the man opened the door. It was Pastor Victor, the follow-up coordinator of the church Ebitobho was attending.

Ebitobho usually attended that church whenever he longed to go to church. He was one of those kinds of people, who compulsorily attend church services on the 31st night of December, which they usually called "The Crossover Night." He believed in starting the year in the presence of God by spending the first thirty minutes or one hour of every New Year in church but the rest of the year; he only attended church services when he felt like. He never went to church frequently. He could count the number of days he had attended church services every year. Nevertheless, on that 31st Night; he would go to church and make a lot of promises to God that he would never fulfill.

"I will not tell lies this year. I will not taste any alcoholic drink again. I will not womanize. I will not fornicate. I will not miss church services this year," and many more promises he normally made at such periods of the year. This had been an old ritual that he usually called 'The New Year Resolution' but he had never kept any of those resolutions. Before the end of the first week of the New Year, he would have already broken them and would have already forgotten that he had even made them.

This year, Ebitobho had already broken all his promises but he had been able to attend church services more often. It was one of those church services that he had met this follow-up coordinator of that church, Pastor Victor, who took his residential address and had been visiting him from time to time.

The sight of the follow-up coordinator stunned Ebitobho. He blinked his eyes in surprise as he recognized him. The sight of the pastor extinguished the wild flames of sensation and the volcanic stimulation that was about to explode. He was transfixed to the upholstery chair, speechless and frozen.

"Good evening, everybody," Pastor Victor greeted.

"Good evening, Pastor Victor," Ebitobho responded while Juliet remained quiet and watched.

"How are you?"

"Fine."

"I have not been seeing you in church these days that's why I came to pay you a visit today."

"Em... Welcome. What can I offer you? Please, come in and sit down. I travelled to the village that was why you did not see me in church today. I am just returning from the village," Ebitobho said.

"Oh! I see. Welcome. Don't worry about that. I am fine. How is everyone in the village?"

"They are all fine," Ebitobho replied.

"I want to go," Juliet told Ebitobho and stood up.

"You can't go now," Pastor Victor replied.

"Sorry, Sir. I was about leaving before you came in. I just came with him to know his place. My mother is already expecting me at home. She sent me to deliver a message to her friend and I have spent so much time outside. Please, bear with me. I will see you another day," Juliet said as she walked towards the door.

"Please, excuse me, Pastor Victor. Let me just see her off to the road. I will be with you very soon," Ebitobho said as he stood up and walked out with her.

"This Pastor has spoilt the show for my desperado," Juliet teased with a smile as they walked towards the gate and Ebitobho laughed.

"I don't know what on earth brought him to my house at such a crucial time of my life when I was licking off the hot juicy plates of kisses from its original source. Gosh! *That guy no try at all! Him don spoil things for me!"* Ebitobho said as they continued to laugh and walked towards the gate. "When next will I see you?" Ebitobho asked when they finally got to the road and stood beside the gate of the Marine Estate and waited for a motorcycle.

"I don't know," Juliet replied.

"That means: it will take me some decades if not a millennium for me to see your face again, right?"

"Do you think I can bear that again?" Juliet asked, laughing. "The wine that is intoxicating you is also intoxicating me. Don't worry; it won't even last for a week."

"I enjoy it when you boldly tell me how you feel. It gives me more confidence to go crazy for you. It also relaxes my anxiety. Well, I pray that I will see you soon else, someone will definitely wear his pant on his head and run into the streets in the name of madness," Ebitobho said, and both of them laughed.

"Don't worry. You will see me soon."

"Ok. Let me take you at your words."

Ebitobho beckoned on a motorcycle that was passing by. There was no passenger on it. Juliet climbed the motorcycle and left while Ebitobho returned to the house quickly, almost jogging. When he returned, Pastor Victor was waiting for him patiently. Immediately he entered the room, they prayed and read some portions of the Bible and Pastor Victor began to preach.

"Bro Ebitobho," Pastor Victor began, "life is too short. When we see it glowing, we may think; it will continue to glow forever. However, the Bible says that life is just like a vapour that will surely disappear someday. When that happens, all that will matter would be; how well did you spend your life here on earth. It is appointed unto man, once to die and after that judgment. If we close our eyes; what will be our fate? I encourage you to take your relationship with God more seriously than anything else in this world. Those things you neglect for its sake will become yours. For the Bible says: seek ye first the Kingdom of God and its righteousness and all other things shall be added unto you."

Pastor Victor talked for about thirty minutes and at the end of his sermon, they joined their hands and prayed again before the follow-up coordinator left. Ebitobho spent some time to think about what Pastor Victor had said to him. However, he soon allowed his thoughts to settle on Juliet.

Ebitobho could hardly sleep that night. He laid on his bed for hours as his memory replayed the episode of Juliet's visit. He wondered how long it would take for them to see each other again. He rolled from one end of the bed to the other restlessly as his mind continued to replay everything that happened.

National Electric Power Authority (NEPA) had ceased the supply of electricity few hours after Pastor Victor left his place. Since he was already in bed and was about to sleep; he had refused to light the kerosene lamp so that it will not generate heat in the room.

He allowed his thoughts to savour his encounter with Juliet. He couldn't think of anything else. He remember how from the very minute they set eyes on each other, it was just joy inexplicable, smiles irrepressible and laughter uncontrollable all the way.

"My encounter with Juliet seems to be a different kind of experience," Ebitobho said to himself. "Is this love or what? I don't usually feel this way about any woman in the past. What am I doing? What is happening to me?" he wondered.

However, as the nocturnal beings continued to sing and celebrate the victory of darkness over the daylight; the friendly gentle virus of sleep invaded his entire being, gradually paralyzing all his immune system, and he closed his eyes in submission to the gentle call of nature and slept off.

Chapter 5

The early morning dry season hot sun began heating up the land immediately it emerged from its eastern grave. It was not yet noon but its heat was intense and dehydrating. Ebitobho had been sweating profusely under the heat. He had been doing some cleaning as the State Government had declared that Saturday as the Sanitation Day of the month.

It was already one week past when Juliet visited Ebitobho. The week was a busy one for him as he went to work in the mornings and went to school in the evenings. He had examinations during the week. The exams were already and vacation had already commenced.

Ebitobho normally worked from Mondays to Fridays. However, he did not usually go to work on Saturdays and Sundays. Those were his work-free days. If he had no lecture on Saturday, he usually dedicated it for all kinds of cleaning.

Ebitobho cleaned the surrounding, washed some dirty clothes, went to the bathroom and took his bath. When he returned from the bathroom, NEPA supplied electricity almost at the very moment he stepped into his room.

"Wow! What a love, NEPA!" Ebitobho exclaimed.

He closed his door, picked the remote of his air-conditioner and switched it on. He went to the television set and switched it on too before applying some cream on his body. He sprayed the house with air freshener, after he had finished applying the cream on his body. He wore a trouser and a singlet, inserted a VCD, which was a musical tape by Mariah Carey before he decided to take a cup of tea and bread as breakfast. After taking his breakfast, he washed the cup and the dirty plates. As he returned to the upholstery chair after washing the plates to enjoy the music but he dozed off.

"Kpoh kpoh!" a female voice, accompanied with a gentle knock at the door woke him up abruptly from his slumber and he sat up.

"Please, come in. The door is open," Ebitobho responded as he yawned, stretched himself and sat properly.

Juliet opened the door, dressed in a brown mini-skirt and a white long-sleeved shirt. She was carrying a new braided hairstyle, and was looking even more beautiful to his eyes. She came into the room, wearing a warm infectious smile.

"Hey! My Queen," Ebitobho said, smiling back as he stood up from the chair and walked toward her. "You are looking so elegant, so gorgeous, so fascinating, so captivating, so tantalizing, so dazzling, so enticing, so tempting, so appealing, so alluring, so charming, so 'biteable' and 'tearable', so chewable and *lickable*, so eatable and drinkable, so...."

"Hey! Bros! Please, keep some of the grammar for tomorrow. I will need them when I come here another day. Do you want to exhaust your limited store of vocabulary today?" Juliet said laughing as they had a warm embrace.

"When I exhaust it, I will buy more voluminous dictionaries and get new ones," Ebitobho said smiling from cheek to cheek. "I missed you so much, my queen," Ebitobho said, giving her several pecks on her forehead.

"Thanks for those romantic pecks. I missed you too, my king" Juliet replied.

Ebitobho disengaged from the close embrace and carried her off the ground in his arms. Juliet chuckled and flung her legs on the air as he carried her and walked towards the bed. He bent forward and laid her on the bed gently.

"Now, you can have a nice sleep my baby," he said patting her on the back. However, when he tried to stand up, she pulled him to herself and he fell on her. He tried to stand up again but she held onto him so he tickled her. Juliet left her grip on him as he began to tickle her. She laughed heartily as she struggled to shift away from him.

"I am pressed. Please, stop or I might accidentally urinate on your bed," Juliet spoke out in the midst of her laughter.

"Please, do. I want to wash a bedspread that has been showered by your royal urine, my queen, so that I could tell our royal children that when I married you; you were still urinating on the bed," Ebitobho responded and continued to tickle her.

"Naughty child! Please, leave me alone," she pleaded. "I am dying. Help!"

"Please die so that I can wake you up with my magic fingers and make some fame," he responded as he continued to tickle her.

"Someone is dying in this room oh! Please, somebody help! I need help oh! I am dying. Help!" Juliet cried gently but Ebitobho continued to tickle her.

"You are wasting too much time. Please, I want you to die immediately so that I will become another miracle worker," he responded with a cruel laughter.

"He is raping me oh! Ebitobho is raping me oh! Somebody, please help! Please, help!" she cried out with a louder voice and Ebitobho stopped abruptly and stood up.

"Hey! Stop that lie. Who is raping you?" Ebitobho asked in his confusion.

"You, of course!"

"But I was not raping you. I was just tickling and playing with you and you know it."

"Where is your courage? In fact, you are very fortunate to have stopped. If not, I would have screamed until all the people in this Marine Estate would have come and gather in front of your door," Juliet said as she tried to tickle him back but he quickly shifted away from the bed.

"I only had some pity for you. I observed that you've already wet your clothes and the bed with your urine?"

"You must be dreaming," she responded, looking at her clothes at the same time.

"Dreaming! Look at the bed. Look at your face. Look at your clothes," Ebitobho said pointing at them at different times. "You've urinated on my bed."

"That's a lie!"

"Look at the ocean of tears on your face! I observed that if I had continued a bit longer; you could have even defecated on my bed," Ebitobho teased and smiled as he walked towards the door, put her shoes inside and bolted the door.

"Naughty child!" she replied, shaking her head. She sat up and wiped off the tears that was flowing down her face and suddenly called for his attention.

"Ebi! My eyes! My eyes!" Juliet moaned gently.

"What happened to it?" Ebitobho asked as he quickly rushed towards her to fine out what had happened.

"I don't know. I can't open it."

Ebitobho was so surprised and confused as he rushed to her side and wondered what might have happened to her eyes.

"Let us wash it with some cold water," he suggested and began to walk to the door.

"No! Please, come and help me by blowing some air into my eyes before we think of another solution," she suggested.

He agreed and walked up to her, held her face close to his face. However, as he was about to blow some air into her eyes, she kissed his forehead, opened her eyes, disengaged herself from his grip and started laughing.

"What was that?" Ebitobho asked with a look of surprised but smiling at the same time.

"I don't know what they call it. However, I call it the ignition for a romantic adventure. I have been planning to do this. Now that I have done it, I feel much better," she said, smiling and winking at him at the same time.

"Then have more of it."

"Nope! I don't want more of it. I have already had enough of it. I don't want my flat stomach to get bigger than this," she replied shifting away from him.

"Are you throwing my words back at me?"

"Yeah!"

"But that was more like a peck."

"But I am satisfied with that. Sometimes, such little things can be very satisfying."

"Hmmm... But I want more of it."

"I am sorry, you can't have more of it."

"You are looking for trouble. You had better give me a good and satisfactory one or I will take it by force."

"You want to take it by force! Come and try me! I will bite off your lips and you will know the person you are dealing with."

"I don't mind if you bite it off. Please, don't only bite it off. Bite it off, chew it, swallow it and wash it down with a glass of wine," he replied and shifted towards her.

"You are looking for trouble," Juliet said.

"You had better give it to me in peace or I will take it forcefully in pieces."

"If you have the guts, come and take it and let's see your strength," Juliet dared him and started shifting away.

"I will so rumple your clothes, you will not have the guts to leave this house until night fall. I am begging you to reconsider this fight you are asking for because you will get much more than you have bargained for right now. Remember, when two elephants fight, the grasses usually suffer," Ebitobho said, pulling off his singlet.

"Haba! Bros, take am easy. E never reach fight nah. Abeg, come and take it. Take enough of it and satisfy your thirsty soul," Juliet replied, chuckling.

"E don pass fight oh. Haven't you heard that the violent taketh it by force?"

Both of them laughed as Ebitobho shifted towards her. He held her face towards his and they soon got themselves buried in the act for some time. That simple act triggered the cloudy smokes of romance that intoxicated them so much that they kept digging in for more from each other. They continued for a while and finally ignited the voracious wild flames of desire in their veins that propelled them to drink from the sacred pot, which finally quenched the potent conflagration.

"I am sorry," Ebitobho apologized as he found her crying. She turned her face to the wall and continued to sob. Tears flowed down freely down her cheek, from the water tank that was in the socket of her eyes. "I was too hard on you. The way you talked, I thought, you were no longer a virgin."

"I told you but you wouldn't listen."

"I thought you were kidding. I am sorry. I am so sorry. I would have listened to you but I was so carried away. I am so sorry," Ebitobho said as he sat beside her on the bed and tried to cheer her up but she used the bedspread to cover her face. He held her hands and tried to pull her to himself. He removed the bedspread from her face but she rolled inside and faced the wall and continued to cry.

"You have taken my pride," she lamented. "You have taken what I have been protecting for my husband. My mother warned me not to visit male friends alone but my stubbornness brought me here today to lose my pride," she sobbed.

"I am very sorry. Please don't talk like that. Your words are piercing my conscience like sharp arrows. I can't bear your lamentation and tears. I thought, you were no longer a virgin. You talked like one who had once had an affair that was why I never listened to your plea. But I promise to make it up to you."

"Make it up to me? That is ridiculous! How?"

"I will stick to you forever. I will..."

"Please, stop there. Don't go any further. I don't want to hear such promises. Keep it to yourself. I don't want to hear it," Juliet interrupted.

"It's fine if you don't want to hear what I want to say. However, I am sincerely sorry, please," Ebitobho said as he shifted towards her and held her to himself but this time she no longer struggled with him.

He rested his back on the bed and held her to his chest for a while but when he began to feel uncomfortable about the way he had placed his neck, he left her and put two pillows under his head. Then, he wiped her tears with his palm and made her rest her head on his chest again. For about twenty minutes, they remained silent on the bed as he continued to stroke her head gently. Then, suddenly, Ebitobho broke the silence.

"What I have done with you today; I have never done it with any woman all my life."

"What do you mean? Are you saying that this is the first time, you are making love to a woman?" Juliet asked impatiently.

"No, that is not what I was trying to say. I mean, I have never deflowered any woman all my life. Since I have taken your virginity – something you've been protecting for your husband – I will make you my wife."

"Your wife?" Juliet asked, sitting up at the same time. "I know that you are only saying that to make me feel happy. You cannot fulfill it and you know it."

"How did you know that I cannot fulfill it? Even if, I have never fulfilled any promise before; I will fight with the very last drop of my blood to fulfill what I have just said – making you my wife. If you think I am kidding, then wait and see me fulfill it. However, my only fear is you."

"Me?"

"Yes. You are the only one that can stop me. If you decide not to marry me, there is nothing I can do."

"Then, throw away your fears because I will not stop you either. I will always allow you to carry out your wish about this matter. I don't want to give my body to any other man. Now that you've had it, I will neither hold back my heart nor my will," she responded, gradually beaming up with her charming smile again.

"Hey! You look so tempting whenever you wear that attractive mask call smile. I feel like raping you." Ebitobho teased.

"Why not just go ahead? You have already done the worst," Juliet replied, smiling. "Excused me! Don't tell me that you are not yet satisfied after you've devoured my virginity like a wild beast?"

"A wild beast? Well, that is what I am. Devoured? Yes, I did because that is what wild beasts usually do. But satisfied? Mmm mmm!" Ebitobho mumbled. "I don't think I will ever be satisfied of having you. Let me tell you a secret. Even your smile serves as a chemical and biological catalyst that stimulates my hunger for you."

"Then, I will never smile at you again," Juliet said, trying to hold back her smiles but ended up in a raucous laughter as Ebitobho tickled her once again.

"Your presence brings me so much joy," Ebitobho said.

"That is the way I also feel. I always feel such an overwhelming and inexpressible joy whenever I am with you. I feel so peaceful and free to express myself. Your presence makes me to discover myself. Something about you just stirs up that strange excitement. I don't even feel like going home, today," she said.

"My dear, this is now your home. Your father's house is just your residence for the moment," Ebitobho said, holding her close to himself again and they remained silent for some minutes again.

"But you have not married me yet."

"Yeah! But my dear, you must also realize that marriage begins with mere thoughts and words. Every relationship began like this before it turned into what others can see. Our expectation shall not be cut short. God will bring it to pass for us."

"Preach on Pastor!" Juliet teased and they laughed.

"I am learning very fast from Pastor Victor, the follow-up coordinator, who came the other day and spoilt the plan of your humble desperado."

"He was very fortunate. The way I saw your face when that man entered the house, I am very sure that if I was not there, you would have devoured forced him and eaten him up."

"No bi small thing! That man no try at all. See as him just bump into my house! Him just quenched our ginger and shattered the journey of our beautiful romantic adventure!"

"He will soon give you back-seat when the seed you've planted in my stomach starts germinating."

"Abeg oh! Trouble no good oh!" Ebitobho replied and both of them laughed.

"What will you do if that happens?"

"Am I not old enough to have babies? You need to see the small boys that have become fathers in the village. I am far older than many of them. Some already have three children. I even felt jealous of them."

"Jealous of them?"

"Of course!" Ebitobho replied laughing.

"Oh! Now I see."

"What did you see?"

"Now I can clearly see that was the reason you were rushing to plant your seed into my body so that I can become pregnant and have babies for you. You have failed. Your plan will not work," Juliet replied and both of them laughed.

"What a preposterous and deleterious proclamation! This is an absurd and outrageous speculation, capable of stirring up strife and felony in a home of love and tranquility!"

"Grammar! Have you started again today? I just thank God that I will be studying Law in the university. All the grammar you are speaking to block my ears...We shall see...Continue. Don't worry. We shall soon meet at the Battle Field of Words."

"Chai! That will be lovely. I can't wait to see that day become a reality. What a day! Just think about it when our children grow up in such an environment, trust me, their schoolmates will be in trouble. In fact, even their teachers will suffer from all these linguistic and grammatical hullabaloos."

"Hmm! That will be so amazing. You know what? I enjoy your wild imaginations."

"Thanks my Angel," he replied smiling at her.

"I just wonder what the future holds for the both of us. Sometimes, life does not deliver what we desire. However, I just wonder what it will be if we are finally joined to live together as husband and wife. I hope things will turn out as pleasant, joyful and full of happiness," Juliet replied thoughtfully.

"My dear, life will always deliver what we desire and aspire to acquire if we don't retire. If we can believe in our dreams and persist; we can actualize those dreams. The Bible affirms it by saying that whatsoever you desire, when you pray, believe, and you shall have whatsoever you desire," Ebitobho said.

"Hmm! My Pastor! Preach! I believe you," Juliet replied and both of them laughed.

"This pastor you are calling me continually, please, take it easy. Who ordained me nah?"

"It was Pastor Victor, who caught you molesting a woman in this room."

"But I was not doing anything when he came."

"Indeed! So why were you breathing so fast and looking so frightened as if you saw a ghost?"

"Naughty girl! You did not see me," Ebitobho replied smiling.

"But I saw you," Juliet replied also smiling. "The righteous is as bold as a lion but the transgressor is as fearful as a thief."

"Evangelist Julie on point! Preach it! What chapter and what verse?"

"Proverbs 28:1," Juliet replied.

"Let's confirm," Ebitobho said bringing out his Bible that was placed on a stool beside his bed. "Oops! Gat yo! From the King James Version, that Scripture says *'The wicked flee when no man pursueth: but the righteous are bold as a lion,"* Ebitobho corrected.

"I am still correct if you paraphrase it," Juliet said laughing.

"My dear, I must acknowledge the fact that you tried. I never knew you could even give it such a try," he replied as he dropped the Bible on the stool that he had picked it earlier.

"But wait a minute! Do you think I don't read my Bible or go to Church?"

"I have not said that my dear. Please, don't put words into my mouth. We are not in the court. I know that you are a legal practitioner. But please, don't drag me to the court now," Ebitobho replied and both of them laughed.

"Are you begging?" Juliet asked.

"Am I begging?" Ebitobho asked too.

"Are you so ashamed to admit it?"

"What do you want to hear?"

"Admit the truth."

"Yes, I am but I am begging honourably."

"Hmm... I just remembered how I planned to make some grey haired people to beg for 'bee' milk but they just enjoyed it freely. They will hear from me next time," Juliet said and they laughed.

"I don't know what you are talking about," Ebitobho said.

"Don't worry. You days of begging are already here. When you start begging continuously like a beggar, you will know what I am talking about," Juliet said and they laughed.

They remained in each other's arms for the rest of the time they spent together, chatting about anything and everything that came into their mind, laughing and chuckling at every little joke. The atmosphere was pleasant and peaceful. The former sorrowful atmosphere had been blown away into an ocean of forgetfulness. Thanks to NEPA that had kept the supply of electricity all through the period that they were together.

Juliet told Ebitobho that she was ready to go home after they had spent some quality time together. Ebitobho walked her to the gate and watched her climb a motorcycle. He stood still and watched until the motorcycle took her away from his view before he walked home slowly to his apartment still ruminating on the time they've spent together.

When he got home, he sat down on one of the upholstery chairs and increased the volume of the television set. Then, he replayed the VCD by Mariah Carey that he was playing earlier. His mind was deeply lost in the thoughts of the past episode. His mind travelled back to the hours Juliet had been with him. He allowed himself to replay the episode over and over again as he remained on the chair.

Chapter 6

It was already evening but it was not yet dark. The bright day light was fading away gradually. Ebitobho was still in his room, pondering on the time he had spent with his new love. He allowed himself to think about the last episode of her visit and wondered what the future hold for both of them. All he could see was a beautiful home, full of love, understanding and joy. He couldn't help smiling at some of the comments she had made when they were together.

"Juliet is such a funny woman, so friendly, understanding and easy to stay with," Ebitobho said to himself. "Look at how we were just laughing and chatting all the way! No dull moments! This is how every relationship should be. A good start will always determine how the future would be. Above all she was still a virgin! I can't believe that such a big girl; so beautiful and friendly could still keep her virginity. Meaning she might not have had any boyfriend. Even though she had, she had the self-control and disciplined to keep her virginity. Wow! I never knew that such girls could still exit in our society in such a corrupt and sinful age. I can't leave her for any other girl. I will stick to her and marry her," Ebitobho said to himself silently with a smiling of satisfaction as he continued to ruminate on his thoughts.

"Hello Mr. Man!" Ifiyemi called and Ebitobho looked up startled. "What has been happened to you? I was knocking at your door but there was no response. I opened and saw you smiling and soliloquizing to yourself. So I decided to wait but you don't want to return from your reverie. I have been standing here for ages, watching your strange behaviour," Ifiyemi said taking a seat opposite Ebitobho. "You didn't even notice when I entered the room! Are you alright? What is happening to you?"

"My dear, I travelled with my thoughts to a distant land where there is only love, peace and joy. I never knew that my eyes and my ears stopped functioning and also travelled with me."

"Welcome back from your strange journey."

"Thank you."

"So what did you bring for me? I have been watching over you like your guardian angel, protecting you from every harm of the enemy."

"Na me send you work? See how you just came in, interrupted and spoilt my enjoyment for that distant land!"

"Ehen! Na so you talk?"

"Well, I can give you the gist of my beautiful experience in that foreign land that I went to enjoy myself."

"Dem dey chop gist?"

"My brother, half bread is better that kpof-kpof. You had better manage what I have. *Dem say, at all, at all, na witch!"*

"Oya, make I hear that your gist. But let me warn somebody. *I no dey give anybody beer today oh."*

"My friend, you are insulting me!"

"I am very sorry, Sah!" Ifiyemi said, laughing.

"Sorry yourself! I am not a drunkard, my friend!"

"I know you are not a drunkard. I was not directing my speech to you. I am very sorry, Sah!"

"Rubbish!"

"Abeg, na slip of tongue oh. I am very sorry oh."

"I will forgive you for today because my mind dey sweet me. Else, for insulting me, you would have appeased me with seventeen bottles of beer and seventeen plates of fried snails before hearing this gist."

"Hmm... Now, I am interested in this gist that making you so happy. Please, let me hear it."

"I travelled to a faraway country, where only dreamers can visit. I saw myself sitting in a large cinema hall; replaying the thrilling and captivating episode of the remarkable time I spent with an angel."

"An angel?"

"Oh yes! My friend, something strange has happened to me," Ebitobho said, shifting forward on the upholstery chair. "My grandfather once told me that every young man with flesh, having some red blood flowing in his veins will put on the strange garment of madness, once in his life. This is the madness that transforms a youth into an adult."

"Hmm... You have started dancing around with your words like a masquerade. My friend, I am not ready for all those grammatic noise. Please, kindly speak plainly to my understanding," Ifiyemi replied.

"A strange wind has blown me away. It came suddenly from the North, then from the South, then from the East and finally from the West. Like dry pieces of dust, I yielded to its sweeping force. Now, it has swept me away to a strange land. This strange wind came gently but swept me away like a tornado. I am helplessly trapped in this gentle but strong wild wind. It is still carrying me away to another unknown destination. Now, I don't know where I am right."

"Your head don dey shake again abi? Please, stop speaking to me in this strange language. It is irritating me," Ifiyemi complained.

"Then, you were not listening to me. You had better listen to me attentively. Put on your listening ears and listen to me more attentively."

"All these novels you are reading is turning your head upside side. You had better stop reading those books before you start wearing your pant on your head."

"But I like it."

"I don't care. Leave your literary world of illusion. I am not interested in your poetic and linguistic jargon."

"That is the real world of ecstasy."

"I am not interested."

Ebitobho laughed, shook his head and continued.

"When you entered the room and discovered that I didn't notice your presence; it was not ordinary. I was in that world of ecstasy. It was so peaceful, full of joy and happiness. The ambience of love was so amazing. I can still feel the strong embrace of the feeble hands of love. My friend, you will not like to come back to this earthly world whenever you travel to that world of fantasy."

"Rubbish!"

"If you have not been understanding me, please be patient. You will soon understand. Just keep on listening and watching this drama that is playing right before you."

"Alright. Go ahead with your madness."

"Well, well, well. Let me come home so that you can partake of this new wine that is intoxicating me. What you saw was a gushing overflow of some hidden and innate springs of emotions, flowing from the large bowl of my pumping machine that is protected in the hidden chamber of my chest. You came in at the exact time, when a thunderous explosion erupted from my hidden chamber like a volcanic eruption and made me deaf and blind. It was ignited by the highly inflammable words of an irresistible and adorable lovebird that visited my nest few minutes ago. I was actually feasting on the thoughts of the sweet memory of her company. The intoxicating words of her mouth had possessed me like opium. That was why I never cared when I was drowning deep into the bottomless deep of my emotional ocean."

"You will never cease to surprise me with your meaningless and useless poetic expressions. The only thing I could pick from your jargon is the word 'visit.' So tell me, who came here? Who was that irresistible and adorable lovebird that visited your nest?"

"I call her the end of search. In fact, she is the last bus-stop of my search for my missing rib. She is the goddess of beauty, the beauty on the face of the female human gods, the beauty of the universe, the epitome of African beauty, the queen of my world, the flower of satisfaction, the stigma of stimulation, an embodiment of admiration, the river of passion, the pasture of productivity, the fountain of peace, the springs of joy, the mother of my children, the...."

"My friend, hold it. Keep your long sermon for the right ears. All I asked was her official name, the name they called her on her naming ceremony. You can use those flattering names to blow up her head whenever she comes to visit you. This is not the first time I have heard such deceptive poetic verbiage from you. Where is Princess, the one whose blood you used as the sacrifice on your bed, to open the door of your house on the first night you parked into this apartment? What about Ebitimi, the one you called the queen of black beauty? What about Roseanne, the one with the angelic voice? What of Doreen, the one you call the busty queen? What of Doris, the one who had the buttocks meant for three women? What of Julian, the one after your own heart? Where is Glory, the one who brought food for you every day? Where is Nnena, Helena, Helen, Janet, Joan, Josephine, Chioma, Ifeoma, Ijeoma, and the rest? *Oh mehn! Guy, you dey worry oh. I never see your type among my friends."*

"Please, don't stop. Continue. Count them. Let me see the length of the number of women that have fallen prey to my paws and claws in the recent past," Ebitobho said laughing.

"Ok! I will continue. What about Tari, the shortest among all of them I have known, who visited you like no other? What about Fatima, who was the fattest among all of them that I have known? What about Sharon, the one with the lightest complexion? What about Itoro, the insatiable lady who almost killed you in bed. What about Beatrice, the one we nicknamed dear Mama? What about Beauty, the lady who never allowed your clothes to get dirty by parking them home to wash. What about Monica, the lady whose parents owned several supermarkets in town. Mehn! You are a bad guy! You deserve an award," Ifiyemi said, laughing.

"Have you finished?" Ebitobho asked, also laughing.

"I have not finished. What about Ere, the one that was here yesterday? The one, you called the mother of your children, the Queen of the Great Island of Ebitobho's Kingdom, the most adorable queen the eye had ever seen, the rare gem of womanhood, the pride of womanhood, the ego of beauty, the crown of your lustful eyes. You have said a lot about her. Where will you place her in your heart, now?"

"My dear friend, all of them have fulfilled their purposes in my life. They were holding brief for the real owner. Moreover, as for Ere, it's already over between us. Our boat sank last night at the middle of the Atlantic Ocean. Can you recover such a boat from the middle of the Atlantic Ocean?"

"Eh! You can't be serious! As far as I am concerned, no woman has ever shown you love the way she has done."

"That is now history, my friend."

"You must be joking, right!"

"There has never been any time in my whole life that I have been ever so serious with my words than now," Ebitobho blurted out with an expression of seriousness written all over his face.

"Well, this is not strange. I just feel sorry for her because I have become so close to her. I don't know what all these women see in you. I wonder what you do to make them fall prey to your pranks. I just keep on wondering why they keep falling for you cheaply and continually flock around you like wild bees. I just feel pity for them sometimes."

"Bros, watch your mouth!"

"I know that the truth stabs the guilty heart with blunt crooked daggers, which would definitely hurt and those who say it are hated for it but how else can I show my genuine friendship if I don't tell you when you are doing the wrong thing."

"I know that I am doing the right thing. I have perceived the tantalizing aroma of true and genuine love and I have made up my mind to taste from that hot pot and eat from it continually until I develop a big pot belly and finally go back to the belly of the earth."

"Hmm... Those words are very heavy! How do you know she loves you more than the way Ere does?' Ifiyemi asked gently.

"A woman wouldn't keep her virginity for a man she does not love. I wooed this girl six years ago when she was still fourteen. I was seventeen then. We became very close friends when I was staying with my uncle. How else do you want a woman to demonstrate her love if not by striving hard to keep her body for her man? As far as I am concerned, the greatest sacrifice for love is keeping your body for your man or woman."

"It could be some parental influence that might have helped her kept her body."

"It is not just parental influence. A girl that has made up her mind to give her body to a man cannot be stopped by any parental influence. Will they follow her everywhere? Keeping your body is a personal choice and decision."

“That doesn’t mean both of you are compatible. How do you know that both of you will make a better pair?”

“I have lived with this girl in the same yard. Everyone in the yard commended our friendship. Even though we were quite young and naïve and never ate the meal reserved for the married. We were best of friends. I have started seeing the same thing again.”

“I am not trying to discourage you about your relationship with your.... Em....”

“Her name is Juliet.”

“Oh! I see! Image the invitation tag Juliet weds Ebitobho... But you should have changed your name to Romeo to make it look exactly like the Shakespearean love story. Then it would be Juliet weds Romeo and both of you would become the Romeo and Juliet of Nigeria. Mehn! I am sure that the whole nation will gather and celebrate such a symbolic union of love.”

“It’s not necessary. The most important thing is that we are happy being together.”

“Please, I am not trying to discourage you about your relationship with your Juliet. I just don’t want you to take a hasty and nasty decision and regret later. Ere has supported you in so many ways. She has been patient with you even when, the hideous demon of womanizing possessed you and you jumped from Jane to Jennifer, from Rose to Rosaline, from Sharon to Charity, from Mary to Miriam, from Cecelia to Felicia, from Debora to Rebecca, from Kate to Catharine and so on; she remained faithful and true to you.”

“Bros, na wetin dey worry you sef? What of the ones wey you dey do nah? In fact, you are the one who taught me to live like this.”

"You did not learn it from me."

"I learnt it from you. When you were heartbroken by Nkem, you said that you will never give your heart to any girl and you resorted to sex workers. You have been with different sex workers since you had that heartbreak. For the past one year, can you count the number of girls that have warmed your bed? You have been bringing them home so I have been seeing them. What is the different between the thing you are doing and the one I am doing? In fact, yours is even the worse. I don't and will never patronize sex workers. Nevertheless, you have been doing it with great ease, without any fear. We are birds of the same feather. You are not any better, my friend. Therefore, you are not the right person to give me any piece of advice on this matter."

"I always admit my flaws. However, you can also attest that I have not broken the heart of any woman."

"Does that make you any better?"

"I am not saying that I am better. I am just saying that you should look before you leap. You seem to take so much delight in breaking the heart of innocent women. You take advantage of their love and hurt them for loving you. That is not fair. It is very wrong. Stick to one woman, my friend. How will you feel if another man treats your sister the way you treat other girls?"

"I have my life to live and my sister has her life to live."

"You had better change your ways, my friend."

"Change and become like you? Are you advising me to patronize prostitutes like you do? Or you want me to be the one crying that a woman has broken my heart? What are you saying?"

"I don't know. Why I am disturbing myself with something that doesn't actually concern me? It is your life. You can live it the way it pleases you."

"Thank you. Now you are talking. I will live my life to please myself just the way you have been living yours to please yourself. Live your life and let me live my life."

"It's alright. However, remember; it is only a good friend who wants to see your progress that can actually advise or correct you. Most times, the person may also have some serious issues to deal with. However, it is his love for you that sometimes make him speak out so that you can do better than he is doing. Remember that you are like the actor that others are watching on a television screen. Those watching may see your mistakes much more than the way you may notice them. One popular adage says that the dancer never sees his back. So if I am advising you, be happy about it even if you do not make amends immediately because it is for your good."

"Wow! That is so touching," Ebitobho replied with a laughter. "Well, thanks for your concern, my dear friend. I will change and become a better me. In fact, this decision is part of that change that you are trying effect in my life," Ebitobho said smiling.

"It's alright. However, that is not why I came to visit you this evening. I came here to inform you that Pastor Victor was here some hours ago. Your door was locked when he came. He saw me outside and told me to inform you that you should try and be in church, tomorrow."

"Thank you for the message."

“Please, ensure that you go to church, so that God can forgive you of all your sins. Your sins are now as red as scarlet and crimson. He alone can wash them whiter than snow.”

“What of your sins, have they been washed whiter than snow? Yours is as black as charcoal and that even makes it worse. Don’t try to remove the spec in another person’s eye when you have a bigger one in your own eye. Is it because I am not counting the different harlots you have been patronizing?”

“Why not count them?”

“I have better things to do with my time. I don’t have a fro-ward mouth like yours.”

“But you have a fro-ward poetic mouth, crafty for deceiving naive women.”

“Don’t start.”

“Oops! I guess that hurts. I am sorry,” Ifiyemi apologized immediately and both of them began to laugh.

“Oh no! Why did I give my address to this pastor? This man is becoming a thorn in my flesh,” Ebitobho complained and Ifiyemi laughed.

“But you are the one who looked for it.”

“But I am tired of his troubles. I want some peace. What does he want?”

“Look at you! Indeed, I can see that you are in big trouble. Your eyes can attest to it. This girl has swept your heart away and sealed it in a hard hidden container in her heart. You had better seek for help from Pastor Victor else, you are doomed. It seems you no longer care about your relationship with your Creator because of this girl. That is quite amazing!"

"Your prayer is working."

"Really?"

"You are a witness today. I like it because I am enjoying it."

"But soon you will say you no longer like it. That is when she will know the real you, the unrepentant father of all womanizers."

"And what will you call yourself, the unrepentant grandfather of all womanizers and a teacher of those who patronize prostitutes? Please, allow me to keep my mouth shut before I make you go home with tears, ok?" Ebitobho said and both friends laughed.

"Abeg, let me leave you alone to enjoy your loneliness so that you can think of your new lovebird."

"Please, run before I count your sins. I know that the hot charcoal of guilt has been burning your heart and you have been looking for a way to escape so that your sins can remain covered," Ebitobho responded.

"Leave me, abeg."

"Who is holding you? Abeg, use the door," Ebitobho said.

"Very soon, you will be looking for me to keep you company. Loneliness will kill you in this lonely house."

"That is a lie. Are you living with anyone in your house? You are also living alone. You are the one that is always looking for a companion. Very soon, you will come back and knock at my door. Go to your house and enjoy your loneliness, overdue bachelor. Your mates are getting married but you are chasing after sex workers. Go and get married," Ebitobho sneered and both of them laughed.

"What are you waiting for, lover boy? Is marriage not good for you? The money you are wasting on these girls would have paid the bride price for one of them."

"The money you are spending on those sex workers, are they not enough for you to get a wife?"

"Na you sabi! Please continue to drown yourself in that ocean of deep emotional thoughts. I am sure she will be thinking of you too. It will be very nice if both of you can think about each other at the same time. That is the miracle of true love. Enjoy yourself, my friend!" Ifiyemi said as he stood up.

"Goodnight, my dear. Make sure you sleep alone tonight. If I see another sex worker in your room; you will be very sorry. Tomorrow is Sunday and you must keep yourself holy."

"Make una see the person wey dey advise me! You have already had enough to your satisfaction. Your stomach is already protruding like a nine months pregnant woman. Are you now advising me to go to bed hungry? Well done. Thank you very much, my good friend."

"I am only trying to advise you so that you can become a better person. I don't want you to be like Ebitobho."

"Thank you so much for your beautiful piece of advice. I am out of here. Make sure you snore like a gorilla. The chimpanzees will be singing for you all through the night, while the baboons will be watching over you as your guardian angels. Fear not, my little monkey."

"Make sure you snore like a rattlesnake. The black mamba will be hissing for you all through the night, while the king cobra will be watching over you as your guardian angels. Very soon, the venom of those crawling beasts will make you sleep peacefully for eternity. Fear not, my little frightened chicken."

"You are such a certified clown."

"I learnt it from you."

"You didn't learn it from me."

"Bros, you have finished all the saliva in my mouth. I am tired of talking. Are you not still tired of talking tonight?"

"Can't you see that I am not tired yet?"

"Who did this to you?"

"My brother, I don't know," Ifiyemi replied and both of them laughed.

"I feel so sorry for you. Please, help yourself. Go and sleep. Thank you and goodnight," Ebitobho said.

"Ok oh! Goodnight, my friend" Ifiyemi replied still laughing, as he walked out of the apartment and closed the door behind him.

Chapter 7

The baby sun crawled out from its dark cave from the Eastern horizon and chased away darkness from the atmosphere into its hiding, broadcasting the arrival of the radiant Sunday morning. Ebitobho was already awake, his eyes were open but he was still enjoying himself on the bed rolling like a baby. Then, he suddenly looked at the wall clock; it was about 6.30am. He rolled down and knelt beside his bed and prayed for about fifteen minutes.

He stood up and dressed the bed after his prayer. Then, he opened the door of his room and swept the room and the surrounding. When he was done, he bushed his mouth, took his bath and began to dress up for church service. As he was still dressing up, his bosom friend, Ifiyemi, knocked at his door and walked into the room.

"Where do you want to go?" Ifiyemi asked as he stood in front of his friend.

"Have you lost your manners? Have you greeted your boss this morning? Where did you get this new bad manners you are trying to exhibit this morning?" Ebitobho asked.

"I'm sorry, Sah," Ifiyemi apologized with a chuckle of mockery and bowed his head in a ridiculous courtesy.

"You had better be sorry of yourself."

"Good morning, Sah," Ifiyemi greeted.

"Good morning, my boy. How was your night?"

"It was fine, Boss."

"Good. Very good."

"Yeye! See wetin dey hungry you!"

"You know I am your boss! Don't forget that else, you will be fired without mercy."

"Rubbish! *Abeg, where you wan go?"*

"Why are you asking such a useless question? Don't you know that today is a Sunday?" Ebitobho asked.

"Oh! I forgot."

"Why won't you forget? If you don't want to go to church, did you think I will also remain in the house with you, Mr. Pagan?"

"Hmm... Wonders shall never end! At last the unrepentant Romeo of the twenty first century has finally given his life to His Saviour because of my persistent fasting and prayer. Thank God that I fasted and prayed for him. Since you are going to Church, I will also go so that I can give thanks on behalf of my dear bosom friend," Ifiyemi said, laughing.

"You must be very drunk, this morning," Ebitobho retorted.

"Yes, you are very correct. I just finished the seventh bottle of *kai-kai* this morning before I came here."

"Please, I don't want sinners to entice me and delay me with unnecessary discussions this morning. Let every drunkard and sinner man, get behind me."

"Hmm! I hope you know that a child of God must not fornicate! What will you do about your new catch, the mother of your twelve children yet unborn, the one who took away your heart, your eyes and your ears in her handbag, yesterday?"

"That is not your business. As you can see I am on my way to church before you came in. Please, you are delaying me. I don't want to go late. Go to your house. Did you come here to put off the flame of my enthusiasm for service today? Satan, get behind me!"

"Abegi! Make I hear something! Even Satan goes to church these days," Ifiyemi replied laughing.

"You are the Satan in flesh. You want to come and stop me from going to church. You have failed. Some of your age mates are already in church. Others are preparing to go to church but you are lazing around, visiting friends so that you can make them talk and while away their precious time. May God have mercy on you!"

"Amen! Thank you for that beautiful prayer. I need God mercies and grace more than anything in this world, my dear. Can you imagine that I have just lost more than twenty thousand naira this morning?"

"What! How did it happen?"

"I brought one girl home last night. After paying her for her service, she still had the guts to steal my hard-earned twenty thousand naira. Can you imagine that I walked her to the gate and came back home before I discovered that the money has disappeared?"

"Serves you right!"

"Is that the best way to show compassion to a friend?"

"You don't deserve any compassion, sympathy or empathy. After all I said to you last night, you still went ahead and did the same thing! Serves you right!" Ebitobho said.

"That is not fair."

"You had better go and take your bath, change into nice clothes and come follow me to church."

"Look at who is inviting me to church? Are you any better?" Ifiyemi asked.

"I am not but no prostitute has ever stolen money from me. This is not the first time this has happened to you. They have stolen your money, jewelries and wristwatches continually too but you will not learn from your bitter experiences. What is wrong with you? Get a decent girl and hook up with her, my friend," Ebitobho retorted.

"What is the use getting a decent girl if she will only end up hurting me after all the love, care and commitment?"

"There are some good girls out there that will not dump you. Don't use one experience to judge all the women in the world. You said this to me and I am throwing it back at you. Go and get a good girl!"

"Don't open your mouth wide to talk to me in this manner! Have you ever been heartbroken? Has any woman ever dumped you? Have you ever been rejected for someone else? Have you ever dated a woman and remained faithful to her for several years? Have you ever proposed to a woman, shown her to your people but she still dumped you? You have always been on the privileged side, breaking the heart of the naïve women that comes your way. So what do you know about mourning a broken relationship for more than a year?" Ifiyemi asked, a bit angrily.

"I know that I am not the right person to talk to you on this subject. However, if a drunkard can speak words of wisdom sometimes, please allow me to speak to you today. You don't have to listen but let me speak. If Nkem dumped you because someone richer came her way, it just tells that both of you were not meant for each other, period! She was not your own. I believe the saying that what is yours will become yours."

"Well, as for me, I don't believe in that saying. I know that sometimes, you can lose what belongs to you."

"You can only lose what belongs to you through carelessness, negligence and ignorance."

"You are wrong. Desperate people can do anything to get what belongs to you. If they are wiser, stronger or richer, they can put up a very strong fight, offer anything in their possession to take what belongs to you. And there is nothing you can do about it."

"Well, I am not trying to force you to believe a plausible saying; I am just trying to make a point with it. If Nkem can be so influenced by money and material possessions to the extent that she could abandon you, then she is not good enough for you. She is the kind of woman that will abandon her man when things get tough. You don't need such a woman by your side. You need someone who can stand with you and stand by you to face the challenging circumstances of life. That's why you must try and forgive her; forget her, forget the past and move on. The choice of resorting to sex workers to warm your bed continuously is not the best option my friend. You are actually endangering your life. In fact, you are destroying yourself. You have to stop it. God has someone better for you but you will not see her if you keep on brooding and looking at your past. Let it go and move on. Someday in the future, you will realize that it happened for your good."

"*Hmm! Make una come see oh! My guy don suddenly turn into a Pastor oh! Chai!* Preach! I can feel your message," Ifiyemi said, and they laughed.

"I am not preaching. I am just telling you what I feel about life. When one door closes against you and you remain at that closed door, you will not get to the other door that has been opened for you. My Pastor once said that if a door is closed against you, God could be saying that what is behind that closed door does not belong to you. But if you decide to force that closed door open; what you will see behind the door may not bring you lasting happiness."

"My friend, when did you suddenly turn yourself into an expert counselor of relationships and love affairs? Wow! That's nice. Keep it up! I am enjoying this discussion. For once, you are talking like a good friend," Ifiyemi replied laughing.

"Thanks," Ebitobho said, laughing too. "I want you to think about it. Don't allow your past to destroy your future. Those who allow themselves to take decisions that are influenced by the pain of their past relationships will only end up whipping the wrong people. At the long run, they will only end up hurting themselves. Please, you have to let go of the past and look for a decent woman that will love you for who you are, or else you may lose something more valuable than money next time. I have not heard any pleasant story about men who picked such ladies to warm their beds."

"Hmm! I hear you, Boss," Ifiyemi said, laughing.

"Don't laugh," Ebitobho said. "I am very serious. Years ago, I heard of a man who carried one of such woman home. She went to the shower and took her bath immediately they got to the house. When she came out, the man also went and took his shower. When he returned to his bedroom, he found a coffin on his bed. He shouted and ran out of the room and called the attention of his neighbours. When they went into his room and saw the coffin on the bed, they also ran out. The man abandoned the room but the woman kept appearing to him. He almost went mad. Finally, some members of his family, the landlord and some concerned neighbours brought some pastors and some preachers and they prayed and carried the coffin outside and burnt it. Then, they prayed for him and set him free from the ghost of the woman he brought home which had been hunting him in his dream every night. The man finally got saved and got married. That horrible lesson made him to remain faithful to his wife all the days of his life. I hope you are not waiting for such a funny experience before you stop what you are doing!"

"This is not the first time I have heard such tales. Those stories were formulated to frighten the fearful man. Nevertheless, those stories cannot put any atom of fear in my heart."

"You don't have to continue until you become a victim of such a horrible experience before you believe and change your ways. There is an old saying that a wise person usually learns from the experience of other people so that he will not become a victim of their negative predicaments. There was another story I heard about a man who brought such women home, but woke up the next morning and saw a dried human skeleton beside him on his bed. For this particular incident, I was told that the man died after seven days."

"I have heard these stories before."

"Really? Yet you still risk your life doing the same thing? I love women and you know it, but I can never go to the extreme of doing the thing you are doing."

"I have told you, they are all lies."

"Well, my friend, I don't know why I am talking to you like this today. I have neither drank or eaten anything this Sunday morning. You had better be very careful. Take precaution and change your ways. Most of the women who do such things are not doing it as ordinarily. Most of them are under in influence of some wicked spiritual powers. Stop exposing your life to the enemy of your soul."

"Nothing will happen to me."

"I am not saying something will happen to you. Nevertheless, I think, it is foolishness if someone sees a trap and decides to walk into it by himself with his eyes open."

"Nothing will happen to me, my friend."

"No one can tell when calamity strikes. You don't know what the future holds for you if you continue like this. It is only the stubborn fly that follows the corpse into the grave. There is a way that seems right in the eyes of a man but the end there-off is death."

"Enough! I have heard you. Thanks for your advice and your concern. I will think about it."

“That’s fine. Do you know that you have taken all my time with this discussion? I am already late. I have to go to church now,” Ebitobho said.

“That’s fine. I am happy that you are gradually taking this church thing very seriously these days. I can remember vividly that you hardly go to church but these days, you are trying. You are changing. I am so happy for you. But my only fear is that you will not allow all these naïve girls to rest. If the change can also affect that aspect of your life; I will be very happy. Then I can attest that this church thing is changing you into a better person,” Ifiyemi retorted.

“I know you will not be satisfied until you keep me here all day, talking with you. My dear, if you are not following me to church, it’s time for you to go to your house, please. I will see you when I return from church.”

“Abeg, I don go oh!” Ifiyemi replied.

He led the way and the two friends walked out of the apartment. Ebitobho locked the door and went to church while Ifiyemi went home.

Chapter 8

The scotching mid-day sun was heating up the elements of the earth as Ebitobho walked home sweating profusely after the Sunday Church Service. Few distances away from his apartment, he saw Juliet sitting outside. She looked at his direction and their eyes met. He smiled at her and she also smiled back at him at the same time. When he got to where she was sitting, she stood up and they had a warm embrace.

"Welcome, my king," Juliet said as they disengaged from each other's arms.

"Thanks, my queen. You didn't tell me you will be coming to the house today."

"Oh! I can see that I am not welcomed here today. It's alright. But please, let me just collect the thing I forgot yesterday and I will go back to my father's house immediately," Juliet said.

"Come on! How could you say that? Who is saying you are not welcomed? If you like, you can come here in the morning, afternoon, evenings or even at mid-night. You are always welcomed here. I have told you that this is your home. I said that because I don't want you to come here and wait for me outside like a stranger because you are no longer a stranger," Ebitobho said, hugging her again and giving her a peck on her cheek at the same time.

"Are you sure?"

"Yes, of course. You are always welcomed here," Ebitobho reassured her and gave her another peck on her cheek.

"Thanks," she said as she also gave him a peck.

"So what did you forget?" Ebitobho asked as he left her and began to open the door.

"Are you telling me you did not see what I forgot?"

"I did not see anything," Ebitobho replied as he stopped opening the door and turned to face her.

"Are you sure?"

"Yes, I didn't see the thing you forgot. I guess you might have lost it on your way home."

"I know I forgot it here."

"That sounds like you deliberately left it behind in a secret place that would be difficult for me to locate," Ebitobho said.

"Why not just open the door and let's look for it! Are you hiding anything in that room? Don't you want me to enter the house?"

"Why not?" Ebitobho asked, laughing.

"Then open the door and be patient. I will answer all your questions when we go inside. Sensitive family matters should be discussed and handled in low tones. Do you want strangers to hear such secret family matters?"

"I am very sorry, your Royal Majesty," Ebitobho said, smiling at the same time as he opened the door.

Ebitobho switched on the bulbs and both of them walked inside. Juliet sat on one of the upholstery chairs. Ebitobho also sat beside her and had a short prayer.

"How are you, my queen?" Ebitobho asked as he finished his short prayer, walked towards the television, and switched it on. He also went towards the air conditioner and switched it on. Then walked towards her again and sat beside her again.

"I am fine and how are you my king?"

"I am doing great. As you can see, I just returned from a glorious church service," Ebitobho replied as he stood up and began to remove his clothes.

"Come here, let me help you," she said, standing up too. "Now tell me, how was church?"

"Splendid," Ebitobho replied with a smile as she stood in front of him.

Juliet removed his shirt and his shoes. Then he took it outside to dry under the hot sun. Then, he returned into the room after a few minutes.

"Em... Baby, now tell me, what did you forget?"

"I forget my property," Juliet replied.

"I did not see any of your property," Ebitobho responded.

"How could you see it? Only witches like I could see it," she retorted with a grin.

"What?"

"You heard me."

"I am not scared even if you are one."

"The expression on your face is already announcing your secret fears. I can see it but you don't have to fear."

"What you saw was not fear; it was just an expression of surprise. I was only surprised about what you said."

"That's ok."

"Please, tell me, what did you forget? Since we entered the house, I have been looking around if I could see what you forgot."

"I am not surprised that you did not see what I forgot. I will tell you a little story so that you can figure out what I forgot."

"Nice. Go ahead."

"My father told me one story. According to him, years ago, when he first got married to my mother, he decided to give my mother a special treat by cooking for her. On this occasion, my mother had actually travelled to the village to see her parents. So on the day she promised to return, he decided to cook for her. He went to the market and bought a big catfish so that he could cook native soup for her. When he had finished cooking, he noticed that he could still perceive the smell of the fish he had used for the cooking of the soup. The smell was so awful and he decided to washed all the dirty plates and clean the whole house. Nevertheless, when he was done, he noticed he could still perceive the bad smell of the fish. So he decided to search the house to locate where the smell was coming from. According to him, he spent a very long time searching for the thing that was smelling in the house but he could not find it. Worn out and tired, he suddenly walked towards the mirror and saw a piece of fish on his nose. It was a sticky substance from the intestine of the fish. He washed it off and realized that the awful smell was no longer there.

When he discovered that the bad smell was actually from that thing that was on his nose, he couldn't help laughing at himself. That is the end of my story."

"Hmm! That was a funny one. Nevertheless, I can't still figure out what you forgot. Are you saying that what you forgot is on my nose?" Ebitobho asked and they laughed.

"Those who listen to the stories of their fathers will definitely become wise like their fathers," Juliet said and they continued to laugh.

"You gat me."

"Oh yeah! Now let me tell you what I forgot. You told me you have given me your heart, right?"

"Sure."

"That is what I forgot and I have come to tear your chest open so that I can collect it and go home with it," Juliet said and they laughed.

"Now I see why you told me the story. I am carrying the thing you forgot right inside my chest that's why I didn't see it. You are such a witty child!" Ebitobho said with a smile, holding her to himself and she rested on his legs.

"I am witty because I am learning very fast from you."

"No bi small thing."

"So what will my king eat, this afternoon?"

"Anything my queen gives to me will just be perfect," Ebitobho answered, still smiling. "I know you like rice. There is some stew in the freezer so you can boil some rice for both of us."

"Wow! That's so nice! I can't wait to taste what you have cooked by yourself."

"I hope you won't laugh at me."

"Why would I want to do that?"

"Well, in case you are tempted to laugh at me, just remember that it was a man who cooked the stew. When you enter the kitchen to cook for me, you can do the domestic magic and make me lick all my ten fingers and if possible, even my ten toes too," Ebitobho teased and they laughed again.

"Don't worry. I will not laugh at you. I will just enjoy the stew the way you have cooked it. The most important thing to me is that you took out time to cook for yourself. I know that most young men don't like cooking. So eating what you have cooked by yourself will give me great delight."

Barely an hour later, the lovebirds sat before a hot plate of rice and stew as the steam from the hot meal ascending into the air gradually. They picked their spoons and sat opposite each other before the meal.

"Can my queen, pray for us?" Ebitobho demanded.

"May God bless this food for us in Jesus name, amen," Juliet quickly blurted out her short prayer without even closing her eyes. Even Ebitobho's eyes were still open when she finished praying.

"Amen!" Ebitobho echoed after she had already said amen and he busted into a raucous laughter.

"Why are you laughing?" Juliet asked with a smile.

"Your prayer just reminded me of a story that our pastor told in church, today."

"What did he say?"

“Hey! My mother told me that talking during meals is a very bad table manner. I don’t want to receive any hot whiplash on my fragile back, please.”

“Who will be flogging you for that?” she asked. “Are you still afraid that mummy and daddy will knock your head as they used to do when you were still urinating in your pant? Well, you don’t have to be afraid because a stronger and tougher mummy is sitting right in front of you and she will defend you.”

“Who is the stronger and tougher mummy that is sitting in front of me?” Ebitobho asked with a serious look, wrinkles drawn all over his face.

“Don’t tell me you are so blind that you can’t even see me! If you are blind, you cannot be deaf at the same time because you have been responding to me all the while.”

“Make una come see stronger and tougher mummy oh!”

“Of course! And you know that!” Juliet responded laughing. “Have you forgotten so quickly, what I did yesterday? Can’t you remember the tedious task of a nursing mother that I performed yesterday?”

“Did you perform any tedious task of a nursing mother, yesterday?”

“I can see that you also have the memory of a suckling and I can’t blame you for that. Do you know what! I never knew that I could be such a caring nursing mother. What a thrilling sensation to have your beloved, supposed grey haired tender baby wrapped in your arms, struggling like a wild beast for some dry milk. Oh! What a feeling! I was so carried away with so much love and affection and I could not resist my innocent baby even though I planned to make him beg for my 'bee' milk with seven drums of tears and seven buckets of sweat," Juliet teased and both of them began to laugh.

"You got me again. It's your day."

"Now tell me what happened in church or else, I will starve you of your favourite 'bee' meal. As a caring and understanding mother, I have already perceived that someone will soon ask for the usual nutritious 'bee' milk."

"Who told you that?"

"I know my baby. Your eyes have been begging for it. I have caught them several times. You had better stop the pretense. It can only lead you into the pison of frustration and bitterness."

"Chai! I don enter serious trouble oh. This one wey you dey study me like book!"

"Can you see that I know where to catch you? You had better tell me what your pastor said or..."

"Or what?"

"You will starve. You will never taste that sweet, dry 'bee' milk again, forever," and both of them laughed.

"Ok. I will tell you after the meal."

"Then, the meal must wait or I will sell my appetite to the wind."

"Ok, your Majesty, you win. Our pastor called the kind of prayer you prayed 'the prayers of gluttons' when he was preaching this morning."

"What! Are you calling me a glutton?" she asked as both of them began to laugh again.

“How could I? That would be a very serious crime against the exalted throne of Her Royal Majesty and that would definitely land my big head within the four walls of the prison yard. The pastor was only qualifying the prayer and not the one praying the prayer,” Ebitobho said laughing and suddenly began to cough.

Juliet quickly poured some water into a glass that was on the tray from which they were eating.

“I am sorry,” she said, handing the cup of water to him. “I caused this predicament for you. Please, I am so sorry,” she pleaded.

“That’s ok,” Ebitobho muttered. “Don’t worry; I I’m fine.”

Ebitobho soon recovered and they continued their meal in silence. After the meal, Juliet washed the plates and swept the floor. When they were through, Ebitobho bolted the door as Juliet came in with the plates that she had washed outside. He wanted to avoid the visit of his uninvited neighbours and friends that could come around and spoil the beautiful moment he was about having with her. He inserted a movie titled ‘Coming to America’ and both of them relaxed on the upholstery chair and began to watch the movie.

“Why do you always like to lock the door?” she asked.

“Have you forgotten what happened the other day, when Pastor Victor came and interrupted the magic flow? Can you imagine that he also came here yesterday when we were inside? Ifiyemi, my bosom friend, told me. I don’t want anybody to interrupt the magical moments whenever you are with me. You are more than the whole world to me. I want my entire being to focus on you whenever you are with me. Nothing else matters to me right now,” Ebitobho replied.

Juliet turned and looked at him. She smiled but did not say anything and Ebitobho made her rest on his legs.

"Baby," Ebitobho continued, "the time I am spending with you is the most precious moments of my life. I can never risk it for any other thing."

"Hmm! Are you sure of what you are saying?" she asked.

"If I lie to you, I am only lying to myself. Since from the moment I ate from that sacred pot, I observed that I could never lie to you. Although, it all started from the very first day we met again. Even if I could tell a lie to anyone; it can't be you. You are now part of my flesh and my bones. I don't know how you feel about me but my love for you is true and genuine and nothing on earth can change it. Believe me, I have never felt like this for anyone."

"I also feel the same way for you. Throughout last night, I could not think of anything else but you. All I longed for was to have another glimpse of your face. All I longed for was to see you and chat with you. Nothing could bring the joy and the excitement you bring to my heart. Nothing could bring the satisfaction and the fulfillment you bring to my heart. I longed for this moment more than food and water and nothing could be compared to it. It was such an urgent yearning that required my urgent attention. It was this strange yearning that propelled me to come here today."

"It's a great feeling to love and be loved," Ebitobho said as he looked at her and smiled.

He was so happy that she also felt the same way. They remained quiet for a long time as they watched the movie. Their eyes glued to the television set but their hearts were not there. Juliet was enjoying every moment rest on him. Ebitobho's analytic memory evaluated and analyzed the degree of her words and utterances. After thinking about them for a while, he broke the silence again.

"I will give you one of the keys to the house so that you can come here at will and have access into the house. I have never given the key of my house to any woman. I have no doubt that I want to spend the rest of my life with you. I have no atom of doubt that you are my missing rib, if there was any missing one. Therefore, I will start treating you as one without any reservation," Ebitobho said.

Juliet sat up, turned and looked at him. She kissed him and he kissed her forehead. They kissed for a while and both of them began to swim swiftly along the wild current of sensation that finally transported them to the sacred land where they drank from the sacred pot and settled matters in the ancient traditional way. When they were done, they relaxed and spent more time talking about their families, traditions and cultural activities.

The sun was setting when Juliet told him that she was ready to go home. He delayed her a bit before he finally decided to let her go. When they have dressed up, Ebitobho handed the spare key of his apartment to her. She thanked him and put it in her bag. Then, he saw her off to the gate as usual, waited until she climbed a motorcycle and left before he returned home.

Chapter 8

The relationship between Ebitobho and Juliet continued to wax stronger and stronger everyday as months passed by. He no longer cared for any other woman except Juliet. He cut off every other relationship and stayed faithful to her. Although, sometimes, some of his old girl friends tried to get his attention but he stood his ground and never entangled himself with any of them. Some admirers also tried to come close but he built a defensive wall of hostility against them. Even his best friend, Ifiyemi, was surprised at his new attitude towards women.

"Oh boy! I never believed that you could ever stick to one girl for more than two months in your life," Ifiyemi said one day as both of them were discussing generally about life. "I would not have believed even if the greatest witch doctor or the most renowned prophet told me you could change like this. What did this Juliet give to her Romeo that he has suddenly become so blind and could no longer see any other beautiful girl around?"

"She did not give me anything," Ebitobho replied.

"Did you want to swear for her?"

"I can swear for her, even now."

"Ehen! I feel very sorry for you. You are in a very great trouble for trusting a woman with your life."

"I haven't trusted any woman before but this one is different. I know she didn't give me anything. It is a pure and genuine love that grew naturally from my heart," Ebitobho responded.

"Well, I am very happy for you. If a woman can change you for the better, then that change is a welcomed development."

"I am glad you can see the positive change. However, it is not a woman that is changing me; it is God."

"Hmm! Praise God for you, my friend. *I know say God hand join for this matter, but, Juliet hand also follow for the matter,"* Ifiyemi replied laughing.

"I agree with you. I am also happy for you. I can see changes in your life. You have started taking church activities very seriously. Most times, I am challenged by your enthusiasm and commitment to church activities. I wish you are a member of my church."

"But come on! If you think I am changing for the better, why do you still want me to join your church? The Church I am attending is influencing the change you are seeing. Thus, there is no need leaving it for another. Remember, we all belong to the same Body of Christ."

"I know, however, if we belong to the same church, we will do things together. That will strengthen our friendship and also motivate out commitment to the work of God. We will become a source of strength to each other in every area."

"We don't need to be members of the same church for our relationship to get stronger. When two people agree, they will definitely work together. In fact, we are already working together, strengthening each other even though we are attending different churches. It even started before we joined the different churches."

"Yeah, I agree with you. But wait oh! I never knew you could sleep alone in your room for almost two month without any girl coming around to spend the night. Wow! Amazing! God is still changing lives," Ebitobho said and they laughed.

"My dear, indeed, God is still changing lives. Only his Word can change people. In the Holy Bible, God declares*: 'a new heart also will I give you, and a new spirit will I put within you: and I will take away the stony heart out of your flesh, and I will give you a heart of flesh. And I will put my spirit within you, and make you to walk in my statutes and you shall keep my judgment and do them.'* So you see; it is God. He is the One changing lives here. My relationship with Jesus has changed my life. Thank you so much for your words of counsel. They were the seeds that brought about the change you are seeing today. Thank you so much."

"You are welcome," Ebitobho replied smiling. "You also contributed to the change you are seeing in my life. I want to use this opportunity to thank you too."

"You are welcome. I am also happy that your relationship with Juliet is waxing stronger every day. I have studied her a bit and I can boldly attest that she is a very nice person: peaceful and very intelligent. I hope you will marry her," Ifiyemi inquired.

"I have answered that question before but since you still want to hear the answer again, I will tell you again and again. From the first day I met that girl, I knew that she was the woman of my dream. She is a true friend, a wonderful companion, a very honest, faithful, truthful and trustworthy person. I think, she is the dream of every man. I have made up my mind long ago that I will marry her. She is the only one that can stop me," Ebitobho said.

"That's nice. I am very sure she will make you proud."

"Thank you," Ebitobho replied smiling.

Apart from Ifiyemi, most of the people who knew about the relationship between Ebitobho and Juliet always said something nice about her. Whenever Ebitobho heard such beautiful compliments, it usually made him to love her even the more. The love between the lovebirds grew so strong that they could hardly stay without seeing each other. Their relationship grew continually and became an admirable one in the Marine Estate. Almost everyone knew about them. Some of the people who were close to Ebitobho were already calling her his wife. One weekend, as Ebitobho went home to visit his parents, he decided to hint his mother about Juliet.

"I have found a daughter-in-law for you," Ebitobho announced proudly as he was discussing with his mother.

"I think you are joking because I have always told you that I don't want you to marry any woman outside our clan. You are my first and only son and I want you to marry from our clan," his mother replied authoritatively.

"Mother, please, I don't want either you or my father to make any decision for me when it comes to this issue of marriage," Ebitobho said with a flat tone that indicated his seriousness on the matter. "I am the one that will live with the woman and my choice will be final. All I want is a woman that will make me happy and if I find that woman outside our clan, please just accept her. No one can talk me into it or out of it. I will not accept any assistance from any one to help me make my choice on this matter. I know you may want to help out of love but please, leave that matter to me. I know the kind of woman I want as a wife and I will choose her by myself, please."

"Oh! I see. Well, I want to see that young woman that has given you such boldness to talk to me like this," his mother said, smiling and shaking her head at the same time. "I will not say anything about this matter until I see her, then I will make my final comment and decision on this matter," his mother responded.

Barely a month after that incident, his mother came to Port Harcourt to spend a weekend with him. She came on a Friday evening and on Saturday afternoon; Juliet came to the house. The door was open so she entered the room without knocking and met his mother sitting on the upholstery chair. She stopped abruptly and greeted.

"Good evening, Mama. I am sorry for coming in without knocking," she said with an expression of discomfort written all over her face.

"Good evening. Na who you dey look for?"

"Ebitobho," Juliet retorted. "I am his friend."

"Come sit down."

"Thank you, Mama," Juliet replied.

She walked towards one of the chairs and sat down opposite her, dropped the things she had brought to cook for him. She sat and NEPA suddenly supplied electricity.

"Ehen!" exclaimed Ebitobho's mother. *"Since I came here yesterday, I never carry eye see light. My pickin, do you know how to on the TV?"*

"Yes, Mama," Juliet replied and she went and switched on the television and the air conditioner.

"Wetin be dat tin?"

"This one na air conditioner."

"Wetin dat one dey do?"

"E dey cool the house so dat your body no go hot."

"Ehen! Oyibo!"

"Em.... Mama, where is Ebitobho?" Juliet asked as the tension between them was cleared a bit by that little conversation.

"Him don go work."

"But him no dey go to work on Saturdays."

"Him tell me like dat too but him say him oga tell am say make him go meet am for office, make dem do one kin quick-quick work. Na him make him go work. Him say, him go come back quick-quick."

"Ok."

"Em... Wetin be your name, my daughter?

"My name na Juliet."

"Na you be di Juliet wey my pickin dey always talk about?"

"Yes, Mama," Juliet replied with a smile, nodding her head at the same time

"Ok."

"Em... Mama, you fit... Em... Em... You fit allow me to cook for Ebitobho? I brought these things to come cook for him."

"You wan cook?" his mother asked.

"I for cook if you go allow me," Juliet responded.

"Oya, go cook. Make I eat your food before I go back to the village," Ebitobho's mother said with a smile.

"Thank you, Mama," Juliet said with a smile and began her domestic chores.

"Which kin soup you wan cook?"

"Na edikaikon soup."

"Ediakon?"

"No. Na edikaikon? This one na Calabar people soup. Dem dey use okazi and water leave cook am," Juliet explained.

"You from Calabar?"

"Yes, Mama" Juliet responded.

"Ok! I go look how you go take cook am. We no dey cook this kin soup for our side. Make I learn am from you," Ebitobho's mother said with a smile and both of them began to cook together.

They talked and laughed as they cooked the soup together. Before they could finish cooking the soup, they have already built a bond of friendship with each other. Everything just went on smoothly. After cooking, they sat opposite each other and began to eat from the same plate.

"I like your soup well-well," Ebitobho's mother complimented.

"Thank you, Mama. I am glad you like it. This is my favourite soup. I like it so much. Ebitobho likes it too."

"My pickin, I like am well-well too," Ebitobho's mother replied smiling. *"My daughter, I don see am say you sabi cook well-well."*

"Thank you, Mama," Juliet responded. "I love the way you receive me. I was so scared when I came in and met you. But right now, I am feeling very relaxed. I am very happy to meet you today," she said and Ebitobho's mother laughed. "I feel very comfortable. I feel so relaxed as if I am talking with my own mother. You are such a nice person."

Ebitobho's mother laughed again.

"You be nice person too. Now, I see wetin Ebitobho see for your body," she said and laughed again and Juliet laughed with her. *"I don receive you as my daughter-in-law. Make sure say you take very good care of my pickin, Ebitobho."*

"I will, Mama," Juliet replied, smiling.

"Thank you," his mother said with a smile too.

"Thank you so much Mama. You have made my day. Thank you so much," Juliet said and they smiled.

Just then, there was a knock at the door.

"Come in," Juliet responded.

Ebitobho opened the door and met Juliet and his mother eating from the same plate.

"Welcome," Both of them greeted almost at the same time as if they had planned it. Both of them looked at each other for greeting him as the same time and began to laugh.

"Mama, *tehmini ke pah ye wah* (what was happening)?" Ebitobho asked with a tone of surprise as he entered the room.

"Nyi tehmini ke ari ye wah (what are you seeing)?' his mother asked with a smile.

"Hey! What is happening, baby?"

"You can see what is happening," Juliet replied, smiling at him too. "I know your stomach has been growling. We will be happy if you can join us right away," Juliet responded.

"This looks like a set up," Ebitobho said and Juliet began to laugh again.

"Abeg, leave talk come follow us eat. We know say hunger don catch you well-well. See as the thing just dey show for your face like say you never eat for days," his mother teased and they all laughed.

Ebitobho quickly washed his hands and joined them. They all ate together. After meal, Ebitobho left the room for them. He stayed outside with his bosom friend, Ifiyemi. While Juliet and his mother spent some time together to chat. When she was ready to go, she called him and informed him. Ebitobho and Ifiyemi saw her off to the gate. When she had left on a motorcycle, the two friends returned to the house and sat outside to discuss.

Ifiyemi had seen Ebitobho's mother the previous day. He had also gone to greet her in the morning and the afternoon. However, before the two friends went into their rooms for their night rest, Ifiyemi still went and greeted Ebitobho's mother. When he had left, mother and son began to chat.

"I liked Juliet," his mother began.

"Thanks, Mother."

"Even though she is from another tribe, I have accepted her. I noticed that she is a nice girl."

"Thank you so much, Mother. I have been so worried that you might not accept her," Ebitobho said smiling.

"I have accepted her and I don't want to see another girl tomorrow," she said smiling.

"Don't worry, you will not see another woman tomorrow. Thank you so much, Mother," he said, embracing her.

Such matters could be very difficult to handle sometimes as most parents still dictated who should marry their son or their daughter. Although he doesn't want anyone to dictate who he will marry, however, he felt that the approval and the blessings of his parents were very important. He doesn't want his choice to bring any issue between him and his mother.

Moreover, as for his father, Ebitobho had observed that the man was not the kind of person that will stop him from marrying the woman of his choice. He had tried to discuss with him in the past to find out his opinion on such matters and his father made it very clear to him that wherever he finds love and happiness, he will give his full support and blessings. Thus, he never cared to hint him about it and decided to keep his mouth shut until the right time when the grand occasion was at hand.

Chapter 9

Barely one year later, Ebitobho became very committed to his church activities. Everyday, he was in one church activity or another. It could be prayer meeting today, choir meeting tomorrow, Bible study the next day and so on. Ebitobho and Juliet had been like fish and water since they started their relationship. They usually spend at least two hours or more with each other within every three days but these days they could hardly spend time together with each other.

Ebitobho could no longer create enough time to spend with her as he was enthusiastically involved in every church activity. She complained but nothing changed. Most times, even though he knew that she was coming to the house to spend some time with him; however, his busy schedules with church activities prevented him from creating time for her. Even when he returned from work and found her waiting for him, he refreshed himself and dashed off to church for one activity or the other. When he refused to create time for her, it began to affect Juliet's consistent visits to his place. Although he still loved her and was still willing to spend his life with her; however, they no longer spent quality time with each other. Before now, they used to talk about everything that concerned them but now they hardly spend time to talk about things that concerned them.

One Monday evening, Ebitobho returned and found her waiting for him. She had already prepared his meal when he returned from work so they ate together. After the meal, Ebitobho went to the bathroom to take his bath so that he could go for prayer meeting. When he returned from the bathroom, he saw her crying profusely, tears streaming down her cheek like a flowing tap. Ebitobho was so surprised and he quickly rushed towards her.

"What is it, my queen?" Ebitobho asked.

"Who is your queen? You cannot deceive me. I am no longer your queen. You are not the person I fell in love with. You have changed. You have so changed you can no longer create time for me anymore. You no longer care about me like you have always done in the past. A lot of things have changed and I perceive, very soon, things will surely fall apart."

"Who told you that? Please, don't say such things."

"I don't need anyone to tell me. I have already noticed that I am no longer important to you. You have proved that to me in the recent past. You don't regard my feelings anymore. What have I done? Where have I gone wrong? I can no longer bear the emptiness I have been feeling these days. Please, forgive me if I have offended you in any way."

Ebitobho sat beside her and tried to hold her to himself but she shook off his hands and continued to cry, her eyes releasing tears like an open tap.

"Please, leave me alone and go to your church so that I will not hinder your relationship with your God. I am only crying to console myself because I am missing someone who is no longer sensitive to my feelings and my desires. I have been coming to this house to spend time with you but for the past months, but you've always abandoned me in this house. Do you think, I came here to look at your house? You leave me here to cry like a baby while you go to church. Every time I come here, you abandon me like an unwelcomed visitor. What did I do to you? Why are you treating me like this? Why are you tormenting me like this? Why are you hurting me so bad like someone you never loved? Why are you frustrating my love for you?"

Ebitobho tried to pull her to himself again but she refused again, and shifted away from him and continued.

"You told me I am more than the whole world to you and that you want your entire being to focus on me whenever I come here but these days; you abandon me every day I come here to be with you. Every day I come here, you will leave me and go for one church activity or the other. Are you the pastor of that church now? Can't you even spare a day for me within the whole week? If you don't want me again, please, tell me plainly so that I will go through that heartbreak, dust myself and continue with my life. If things continue like this, I doubt if you will ever create time for me and your children if we even get married in the future. How could you be treating me like this? You told me I am part of your flesh and your bones. Will you deprive yourself of something that gives you the greatest happiness and joy in life? What have I done to you that you are treating me like this? Please, tell me."

“Baby, it’s ok,” Ebitobho said as he tried to pull her again to himself but this time she relaxed on his laps and continued to sob. He allowed her to cry for a while so that it could relief her of the emotional heaviness in her heart. She continued to express herself as she cried in his arms but he remained silent and listened to her.

Ebitobho could not withstand her tears. His conscience continued to blame him as he listened to her. She meant a lot to him and he doesn’t want to be the cause of her tears but he also wanted to have a better relationship with God. He was so confused of what to do as his relationship with God meant a lot to him, and even his relationship with her also meant a lot to him. He was still determined to make her his future wife. He observed that if he decided to grant her request by spending more time with her; he would sacrifice some of the times that he was supposed to be in church. Such times of intimacy could also lead them to the sin of immorality. That was one of the reasons he had been trying hard not to spend too much time with her. He remained quiet and thought of what to do next.

“My queen, I have not changed my intention of marrying you and I will never change it. I just want you to be patient with me for a while.”

“I have been patient with you all this while. Now, I am tired of being patient. Can’t you sacrifice just one day for me within the whole week? Every day, it is one church activity or the other. Do you think I don’t like going to church the way you do? Do you think I don’t have anything to do with my time? You always make me feel that I am hindering you from serving your God that’s why I have been quiet. I know that some of the things you are learning in church will make you better husband and father but does that mean; you should sacrifice our relationship for your church activities? If you can no longer create time for me; then, you are no longer interested in me. Our relationship became this strong because you were always there for me and I have also strived to be there for you always."

Juliet suddenly paused and gave out a heavy sob before she continued.

"You seem to forget that I am also forfeiting other things to be with you but you are not ready to sacrifice your time for me. It seems that you no longer value this relationship. Well, you can go to your church. I no longer want to hinder you from rendering your services to your God. I will go to my father's house since I am no longer welcomed in this house. When you are ready to spend more time with me, you can come to my father's house and inform me. I will be waiting patiently for you. Good bye for now," she said with a tone of finality.

She stood up, picked her handbag and walked towards the door but Ebitobho held her. She struggled with him for a while but he held and pulled her to himself. When he didn't let her go, she threw her bag on the upholstery and began to cry afresh, beating him gently on his chest.

"Why are you doing this to me? Did I make a mistake for falling in love with you? Where is that your caring heart you once had? Where is that loving personality I once knew and loved? Why have you thrown away your tender heart? When last did we gist and play? You hardly care about my emotional appeals. You are no longer sensitive to anything that concerns me. You are gradually becoming self-centered. Is this the way I am going to lose you?"

“You are not losing me. Things are not the way you think, my queen,” he responded calmly.

“Things are not the way I think but they will soon turn out and become the way I think. You can’t cover up for too long. Well, it’s alright. I want to go home,” Juliet said struggling to break free but he still held her to himself.

“My dear, every problem has a solution. Please, sit down and let’s talk over this. You can’t go home like this. I still love you and care so much about you as I have always done. You still mean everything to me in this world,” Ebitobho said.

“That was before,” she responded. “It is obvious to me that things have changed. Actions speak louder than words. Your hidden thoughts are already playing out in your attitude towards me,” Juliet said.

He has strived all these years to ensure that she did not cry because of him. He has always endeavoured to make her happy. Seeing her cry because of his inability to create time for her in the recent past made him feel very bad. He wiped her tears with the back of his palm and carried her like a baby to the bed. He laid her gently and laid beside her. They remained silent for a while before Ebitobho began to talk to her again.

“I am very sorry, my queen. I have caused you so much pain and tears recently. I feel very bad for making you go through all the things you have been going through these days. My conscience blames me for it. My spirit, soul and body condemn me for it. I am sorry for neglecting you. I will make it up to you. Please, stop crying. Your tears break down my entire being. I can’t bear it. Please, I am sorry.”

Juliet continued to sob. After a while, she remained quiet and relaxed in his arms as his fingers continued to crawl gently from her long dark hair to the groove of her back. Steadily but gradually, the magic flood of sensation overwhelmed them and both of them began to swim simultaneously in the massive ocean of those thrilling waves that finally took them to the crest of the ancient sexual adventure.

Chapter 10

Ebitobho and Juliet began to live normally after that incident. He ensured that whenever she came to his place, he was always there for her. Any day he planned to go to church, he ensured that he gave her quality attention the few minutes he spent with her. However, three months later, Juliet got an admission into the University of Lagos to study Law. She brought the news to him one weekend and travelled to Lagos two weeks after.

The distance between Port Harcourt and Lagos made things difficult for them to see each other. Thus, in his loneliness, Ebitobho soon committed his time and resources enthusiastically to the activities of his church. He gave his time, money and even his material possessions to the advancement of the things done in his church.

One Sunday morning, his best friend, Ifiyemi saw him and a young man parking some electronics into an open van. Ifiyemi walked towards the scene to find out what was happening. When he arrived at the scene, he saw that they have already carried the refrigerator, the television stand, the television set, the audio set, and the video players into the van.

"Ebitobho, what is happening? You are parking and you didn't care to inform me about it?" Ifiyemi asked as he stood beside the van as Ebitobho and the driver were trying to arrange the electronics in the van.

"I am not parking," Ebitobho responded.

"Are you sending these things to the village?"

"No."

"Then, where are you taking them to?" Ifiyemi asked.

"Anywhere," Ebitobho responded.

Ifiyemi remained silent and watched his friend and the driver as they arranged the electronics properly. After arranging the electronics properly in the van, Ebitobho and the driver went back to the house and Ifiyemi followed them. When they went into the room, they began to pull out the window air-conditioner. Ifiyemi stood beside them and watched them for a while before he spoke out again.

"Ebitobho! Where are you parking these things to if you are not relocating or parking to another apartment?" Ifiyemi asked impatiently.

"I have told you that I am not parking to another apartment," Ebitobho responded as they pulled out the window air-conditioner and took it into the van. Ifiyemi followed them silently like a supervisor. When they had arranged the air conditioner in the van, Ebitobho returned to the house while the driver opened the door of the driver's seat and sat there to wait for him.

When Ebitobho was out of sight, Ifiyemi walked towards the driver, greeted him and began to interrogate him.

"Bros! How are you?"

"I am fine," the driver responded.

"Did you come from the village," Ifiyemi asked.

"No," the young man responded.

"Are you one of his brothers from the village?"

"No. I am not his brother. I am the owner and driver of the van."

"Ok. I am sorry for bothering you like this. I don't know why my friend does not want to tell me where he is taking these things to. We have been very good friends for several years now. We have no secrets but I am wondering why he has refused to say anything about what he is doing. Do you know where he is taking his property to?" Ifiyemi asked.

"Well, your friend told me he wants to take them to his church."

"Oh! I see. Thank you very much," Ifiyemi said.

He stood with the driver for a while then, he left him and went to meet his friend, who was still in his apartment. He walked into Ebitobho's room and met him preparing to go to the bathroom.

"When did you start hiding things from me?" Ifiyemi asked as he walked into the room.

Ebitobho remained quiet and refused to answer his friend.

"Well, you don't have to worry; the driver has already told me. I know you don't have any conviction about what you are doing. You are so confused you don't even want to talk about it. I just wonder who is forcing you to do what you are doing."

"Nobody is forcing me. It is a personal decision."

"Ok. Good. Now, tell me. Why are you taking your property to the church?" Ifiyemi asked.

"Ifiyemi, as you can see; I am not in the right mood to argue on this subject with you now. Can't you just advise yourself to keep your curiosity and your questions for another time? As far as I am concerned, you can't be of any help on this matter. You can only function as a bunch of distraction and discouragement because you can neither assimilate nor comprehend such deep spiritual matters. It is a divine secret for a selected few, who have made up their minds to abandon their human wisdom and philosophies and have decided to take the Word of God as the final authority in their lives. I don't need to explain anything to you because it is beyond the shallow analysis and comprehension of human wisdom."

"How do you know I will distract or discourage you? How do you know I can't say anything reasonable on this matter?"

"We belong to different spiritual worlds, my dear. Those in your world will only see my action as foolishness and will laugh me to scorn but those in my world will see it as a giant stride of faith and will applaud me for such a remarkable decision and action. I am not trying to underrate your insight into spiritual realities but I know my actions, decisions and mindset on this subject matter will sound very foolish and ridiculous to you. However since you have been insisting to know, I will tell you. After telling you, I will not respond to any further interrogatory question from you. I am taking them to church. I want to sow those property as a seed offering into the life of my pastor," Ebitobho said.

"What? Did I hear you well? Did you say you are sending those things to your pastor?"

"Ifiyemi, you wanted to know where I am sending my things to and now you've known it. As you can see, I was about going to take my bath before you came in. Moreover, the driver is waiting for me outside. Please, I will really appreciate it if you can excuse me now. I want to take my bath," Ebitobho said and he walked out of the room.

Ifiyemi could not leave the room when Ebitobho walked out and went to the bathroom. He was so shocked. He sat down quietly and waited for his friend return. Ebitobho returned few minutes later, tying his towel around his waist.

"My friend, we learn everyday and I am ready to learn from you. I am asking this question because I am shocked and confused. Why are you doing this?" Ifiyemi asked.

"I invited you for our church programme but you refused to attend. Now, you want me to explain why I am doing what I am doing. Well, if you want to understand why I am doing what I am doing; you can go home, prepare and come join me in church this morning. You know where my church is situated. I am inviting you again. Today is the last day of the programme. Come and hear raw and undiluted words that will catapult you to another level in your finances."

"Sorry, I can't make it today. We have a combined Zonal Thanksgiving Service and I will be functioning in one of the group presentations," Ifiyemi said.

"Fine. Then, keep your questions for another time. We can talk about it when we return from church later in the day."

"It's alright. See you later. Do have a beautiful time in church," Ifiyemi said, stood up and left the room.

Ebitobho dressed up quickly, carried his Bible, locked the door and walked towards the waiting van. He opened the passenger's seat and sat down. The driver ignited the engine of the vehicle, and they drove off to church.

Chapter 11

It was Friday evening; about one month after Ebitobho had taken his things to church. He was resting on the upholstery chair in his room when he heard a gentle knock at the door. Before he could respond, Juliet opened the door and walked in.

"Wow! Who is that? Who am I seeing? What a pleasant surprise! Welcome sweetheart," Ebitobho said as he stood up from the chair and began to walk towards her.

Juliet had returned from school to spend some time with him. It was the first vacation of her first year in the university. Being away from Port Harcourt for more than three months, she had decided to come straight to his place, so that she could spend a night before going home Saturday evening to make up for her absence.

"Honey, what's happening? Why is the house so empty? Where are the electrical appliances?" Juliet asked impatiently when she noticed that all the electrical appliances were no longer there.

"Please, calm down. You just arrived."

"I know but I need a little explanation to calm my curiosity. Are you parking from this apartment?" Juliet asked impatiently as she looked around again.

"Take it easy, my dear. You just entered the house and we haven't even greeted each other. Why not take a deep breath? I will tell you everything that has happened in this house," Ebitobho responded.

"Alright," she said.

"You are welcome, my queen" he said as they engaged in a warm embrace.

"Thank you, my king. Please, bear with my impatience. I can barely wait any longer. Please, tell me. What is going on? What has been going on? Where are the electrical appliances? Are you parking to another accommodation?" she asked again as their hands were still wrapped around each other.

"Well, nothing is going on. I am neither parking nor relocating," Ebitobho replied.

"Then, where are the electrical appliances? Where have you taken them to? Did you send them to the village?"

"No. I have sown them as a 'dangerous' seed offering to the pastor of my church," he replied.

"What!" Juliet exclaimed and disengaged from his embrace immediately. "Please, tell me, it is not true. Please, tell me you are just kidding."

"I am not kidding. We were celebrating the birthday of our pastor and I had no money on me at that time. So I took the electrical appliances and sowed them into the life of my pastor as a 'dangerous' seed offering for a supernatural breakthrough."

“I can’t still believe this. Please, tell me, it is not true. Tell me you are just pulling my legs.”

“How can I lie to you?” Ebitobho asked. “I have told you I can never lie to you. Why will I lie about what I have done?”

“Ehen! So you mean, you carried the air conditioner, the refrigerator, the television stand, the television set, the video player and the radio set to church and gave it to your pastor! This is incredible!” she said as she shook her head and began to pace around the room for a while before she sat down dejectedly on the upholstery chair.

“Calm down, my dear,” Ebitobho said.

“Baby, what has happened to you? You have taken this thing to the extreme. You have become too fanatic about it. Just these few months that I was away, you’ve succeeded in empying the house. I am just wondering what you will do if you are given a year to do your thing your way.”

“Why are you saying that?”

“Every woman wants a man she could depend on financially, emotionally and spiritually. A woman wants a man who could not be easily brainwashed and influenced. A woman wants a man who can fend and protect her home. If you asked me to sincerely tell you how I feel about what you have done; I will tell you I am very disappointed at what you have done. Instead of giving your property, you could have given money.”

“I told you earlier I had no money on me that was why I decided to give the electrical appliances.”

"Baby, God knows your heart. He knows everything about you. He knows you don't have any money on you to give at that time. You should have waited until you have the money to give."

"My dear, sometimes, giving requires urgency. We don't only give when things are convenient for us. Most times, the blessings of giving usually manifest when we give at such inconvenient times. God is not willing to do without a prompt to do it giver. He that soweth sparingly shall reap sparingly and he that soweth bountifully shall reap bountifully. God is not mocked; whatever a man soweth, that shall he also reap. This could be my season of sowing. The season of harvest will surely come. The Bible says that as far as the earth remains, seed time and harvest time shall not cease."

"*Chai!* I am convinced you don't even have a good understanding of what you are quoting.

"How could you say that? I understand what I am quoting."

"You have been brainwashed and indoctrinated," Juliet said, shaking her head.

"I am not. I just acted on the word of God."

"When the Bible talks about seed time and harvest time, does it talk about giving your electrical appliances as offering to a pastor? What I understand from what you have just quoted has nothing to do with giving your electrical appliances or possessions as a seed offering. That 'seed time' means seed time. You may give it other interpretations but what it was addressing was planting season. I know that some people now quote that verse of scriptures and use it to achieve certain personal aims but I don't expect you to fall so cheap."

"I haven't fallen cheap for anything. I just acted on the word of God and I know I will definitely reap at the fullness of time. God is not mocked, for whatever a man sows that shall he also reap," Ebitobho said.

"Now, tell me; what did you sow? Is it corn, yam, beans, mango, maize or rice that you are now expecting a harvest?"

"I sowed my property that I bought with money. Those property represent my sweat and my hard-earned money. So I sowed the financial value and the worth of those property. If the value of those property is a hundred thousand naira to me, then that is what they represent."

"Don't you think it is ridiculous that one could go and plant electrical appliances in a farmland and expect to reap electrical appliances? Is it not ridiculous for one to take naira notes, put them in the ground as seed, and expect to reap naira notes? The seed time to a company worker is when the person goes to work and renders his services to the company that had employed him. The harvest time for the company worker is the salary he receives at the end of the month. For those who render services, their seed time is the period they rendered their services to their employers. Their salaries and wages are their harvest. For the employer, what he invests in the company is his seed and the profit from the company is his harvest. Seed time for the farmer in the village is when the farmer goes to the farm and plants corn or any other crop. Harvest time is when the corn or any other crop grows to bear fruits and become matured for harvest and the farmer goes and harvests them. If you ask me, I will tell you that giving out you money and your personal belongings cannot make God bless you or not bless you. The truth is you don't have to do anything to be blessed in our dispensation of grace. You are already the blessed. You have been blessed with all spiritual blessings. You are an heir of God, joint heir with Christ, inheritor of the earth. All the blessings you can ever imagine has been given to you freely in the realm of the spirit. You have been qualified to enjoy it by the finished works of Jesus. All you have to do is just have to bring it out with faith."

"The Bible says, give, and it shall be given unto you, good measures, pressed down and shaken together shall men give unto your bosom. That is the Word of God. I believe it and I have acted on it. And surely, it will produce result in my life."

"What are expecting to reap? Are you expecting other insatiable human beings, who desperately want to take even the little in your pocket to come to your house and give you their hard earned money, just like that? Things don't always work like that. It may may happen sometimes but may not happen always. You are an under-graduate, studying English Studies and Literary Studies in the University. You have heard of propaganda; how people use words to make people do their wishes and desires. I thought you have expanded your scope of knowledge, understanding and reasoning to a level where people could no longer influence you and make you become a victim of such deceptive selfish teachings. How could you have fallen so cheap? How could you fall prey to teachings that will only take from the poor and give to the rich? I don't subscribe to those teachings. "

"I don't like what you are saying. How could you think like that? I didn't give to man but to God. I acted on His Word and not on any man's word. I am not expecting any man to reward me but God; for he is the faithful rewarder of those who diligently seek Him. I know I will definitely reap at the fullness of time," Ebitobho responded.

"Where will you reap your harvest? You neither planted maize nor any other food crop. From where will you reap your harvest when you neither invested your money nor rendered any service to any establishment? Are you telling me you will go to the altar and reap the blessings? When God gives you a job, is that not the blessing? Is the money from the job not the blessing? Are the things you buy with the money not from the blessing? How could you take it, give it to someone who has more than enough, and expect God to bless you again when he has already blessed you? When he gave you the power to get wealth but you give it away because of your ignorance, will you say God did not bless you? Why are you looking for the blessings when you've already been blessed with a nice job that has given you the means to get those property that you have given out? Is that not a clear example of poor management of the blessings of God upon your life? Don't you think that your expectation for a harvest is a display of foolishness?"

"Well, the things of the spirit are always foolishness to the human mind. When the Bible says that give and it shall be given unto you; doesn't it sound foolish? When the Bible says lay your hands on the sick and they shall recover; doesn't it sound foolish? When God told Moses to stretch forth his hands towards the Red Sea to divide it; doesn't it sound foolish? My dear, the actions of faith on the Word will always sound foolish to the human minds. I have told you to relax your mind. When the fullness of time comes, when we begin to reap the multiplied harvest, you will forget the pain of sowing and will rejoice. Remember, the Bible talks about a harvest that is pressed down, shaken together and running over shall men give to the bosom of the giver."

"I don't think God blesses people because of what they do, or didn't do. The Bible says, for God so loved the world that He gave His only begotten Son that who so ever believes in him should not perish. Another scripture says if God could not withhold his son, Jesus Christ from coming to die for us; what then will He withhold from us? He loved us even when we were yet sinners. If God blesses you because of something you gave sacrificially to qualify for his blessings; how then has He demonstrated his love towards you because you already qualify by your works? God loves you and me unconditionally. Why are you trying to qualify with your works? The Bible says, if Abraham was justified by works, then he would have had something to boast of; but not before God. If the blessings of God had come on Abraham through obedience to Law, then it no longer came because of a promise. But, as a matter of fact, God has granted it by grace to Abraham in fulfillment of His promise. It is not our works that qualify us for God's blessings. God has already blessed us with all things that pertains to life and godliness in Christ. Thus, I don't think we should give with the intention of making people give to us. We ought to give to express the love of God. We are not supposed to give to qualify for God's blessing because we have already been qualified by the righteous works of Christ. We are His beloved children, heirs of His inexhaustible wealth and riches. If someone teaches you to give to qualify for God's blessings, then that person is teaching you not to recognize the grace of God. I think, we ought to give being motivated by the love of God; not as a means of getting God to do something special for us. As far as I know, He had done all He was supposed to do in Christ."

"My dear, grace does not nullify works. Indeed, Abraham believed God and it was counted for him as righteousness. However, have you forgotten that Abraham also sacrificed his son? Isaac was the seed Abraham sacrificed that brought about the blessed lineage of the children of God. We do not give to qualify for God's blessings. We just act on God's divine principles of prosperity."

"But that is exactly what you've done even though you don't accept it," Juliet said. "Let me tell you a story that one of my course mates told us in class. There was a pastor of a particular church, who declared to the members of his congregation that they will build a larger church auditorium for God. He selected some people as members of the building committee. The financial secretary of the church was made the chairman of the building committee. The financial secretary knew all about the financial state of the church and when everyone was given the opportunity to give for the building, the financial secretary closed his account for the building project. Barely one month after the financial secretary had closed his account for the building project, the pastor of the church dedicated a brand new Toyota Jeep. On the day of dedication, the pastor testified that a Christian Organization had sent them some thousands of dollars from a foreign country. The financial secretary later discovered that the money he had used to buy the jeep was the money sent by that foreign organization. The financial secretary felt so disappointed by his attitude. During a committee meeting, the financial secretary of the church, who was the chairman of the building committee, confronted the pastor. The pastor became very angry and the meeting almost ended in a physical combat. The financial secretary resigned and handed over every church document his possession and left the church."

"That pastor is still a babe in the things of God," Ebitobho responded.

"You seem to have closed your eyes and your ears about what is happening in churches these days. That is just a glimpse of what is going on in some churches. Preachers now use the Word of God to achieve their personal motives."

"I will face my judgment and they will face theirs. If they misuse church funds; well, that's not my business. I will still do what I am led to do," Ebitobho responded.

"They will tell you to contribute to projects that would become theirs. I have heard of preachers who told their congregation that they want to buy a land for the church and the members contributed to acquire those lands and the lands became the preachers' property. I have heard about preachers who told their congregation that they want to build school and the members of their congregation contributed to it, thinking their children will benefit from the project but at the end, the poor members of the church could not afford the expensive school fees of the school that they have contributed and built. Years ago, it was churches that helped to build schools. They assisted in training those whose parents could not afford to send their children to schools. But nowadays, when they use the members of the church to build schools, estates, television stations and other lucrative business ventures; the proceeds from those establishments only contribute to the luxurious life style of some selected people who head the affairs of the church."

"Baby, this Law you are studying in school is getting into your head," Ebitobho responded.

"Please, forget what I am studying in school and pick the elements of truth in what I am saying. Many preachers now turn their congregation into their money minting machines. While the members of their congregation suffer throughout the month to earn some money, the preachers study their Bibles and pick up verses of the Scripture to manipulate and compel them to give all their salary as seed offering, and then they make them to expect some miracle from God. They therefore take what you have and then make you to force God to do some quick miracle. When those quick miracles do not take place, they still blame you and say you don't have faith. But I wonder how someone who doesn't have faith could act on the word of God."

"You seem to be against giving."

"I am not against the idea of giving but I am against the way you are doing it. I don't like it when people give unwisely and expect a miracle from God. When they did not see the miracle they are expecting, they think God has failed them. However, they forget that they were the ones who had acted unwisely and misused the resources that God has given to them."

"I never acted unwisely," Ebitobho responded a bit angrily.

"But you did. God blessed you with a job and through that job you were able to furnish your apartment to make life a bit comfortable for you. But what did you do? You packed all those property and gave it to someone who don't even need it. If you go to his house, I am very sure that those things are packed somewhere, underutilized, abandoned or even scrapped. Now you are praying that God should rain down money like manner for you from heaven. You are now praying for a miracle which I call magic. I look at you and I can see that you desperately wish to replace the things you have given out. How could you give what you needed to someone who doesn't even need it, yet you are telling me you never acted unwisely? I respect you so much that's why I'm even using the word 'unwise' else I would have used something even more derogatory. I must confess that I'm not impressed by what you've done. Please, in the future, don't allow yourself to become a victim of such deceptive prosperity teachings, aimed at making the rich get richer. I hate it when leaders manipulate those they lead in order to take from them. I get furious whenever I see influential people manipulating the deprived in order to take from them. Sadly, such despicable things now happen in religious circles. Truly, if you had seek my opinion before giving out those property, I would not have allowed you. Since you joined that religious organization, how many of them have given you money or any form of gift?"

"Now listen very carefully," Ebitobho said angrily. "I can no longer watch you become a source of discouragement to my faith. You complain about everything I do to have a better relationship with my God. I am fed up with this relationship and now I want us to take a break. I owe my life to God, the One Who created me and not to you. If I die today, I will not give any account of my life to you. The relationship I have with you has been making me to do a lot of things that I don't want to do again. Now, I want us to take a break. When I am ready to get married to you, I will come and see you and your parents."

"Did you just say that you're fed up with me, and that you want us to take a break, because I am trying to advise you?" Juliet asked tearfully.

"Honestly, you are becoming a source of discouragement to my faith and I am tired of that. I have been taking it lightly with you but now I can no longer bear it. I think it is high time I stopped you from being a discouragement to my faith. I want us to take a break so that I can commit myself fully to the work of God and prove the Word of God for myself," Ebitobho responded angrily.

"Baby! What are you saying?"

"You heard me and I am very serious about every word I have spoken. I want us to take a break. Stop coming to my house for now, because you are becoming a source of discouragement to my work of faith and I can no longer bear that."

Juliet could not withhold the tap of tears that was flowing down her cheek from the reservoir of her eye socket. She quietly picked her bag and hanged it on one of her shoulders as the clean tap of tears flowed down to her cheek freely.

"I am very sorry for becoming a source of discouragement to your work of faith. I was only trying to advise you based on some of the experiences of my own father. My father was a good giver and a helper of many. He helped his relations, friends, colleagues, acquaintances and even strangers. The helped people financially and materially without minding if he had enough for himself and his family. Sometimes, my father went the extra mile of borrowing to assist people. When he lost his job and started experiencing some financial problems, most of the people he had taken extra step to assist never assisted him. We suffered for several months before he was able to secure another job. I wish I had enough time to tell you about some of the pathetic experiences we had from friends and relatives during the period he was out of job. I look at the things you do and I see that you are making the same mistakes. I wish you had a listening ear and an inquisitive heart to find out more about the pathetic experiences we had when my father lost his job. I can see that you have not experienced any hardship in your life," Juliet paused, cleaned her tears and continued.

"Let me ask you few questions. When you look at me, will you classify me as a greedy and selfish person? When you look at our past, can you recall any instance I withheld anything from you? Have I not been generous to you in my little way? Why do you think I don't want you to give to people when the need arises? When you met me, I was a virgin. Don't you think, one of the reasons I was able to keep myself was because I had some fear of God? Do you think you are living a better moral life than I am? No other man has crossed my legs since I was born. Answer this question by yourself silently. Am I the first and only woman you've ever slept with all your life? What makes you think that I don't want you to have a good relationship with God? I have become your enemy because I tell you the truth. I have become a source of discouragement to your faith because I advise you to be cautious with your giving. It's ok. I am sorry," Juliet said as she wiped the tears flowing freely down her cheek.

"Let me tell you something; any man who cannot fall back on another means of income immediately he loses his job is doomed for hardship. I can see it coming but you have been so blinded by your beliefs. I know you will never see it because you have been indoctrinated. I only advised you because there is something I am seeing that you are not seeing. I could be wrong but I pray that you always have more than enough to give. I pray that you will never come to a point in your life where you start looking for help from people. I pray that your faith works for you always. Let it produce the remarkable results you have desired and expected, else you will also learn your lesson like my father in a very hard way," Juliet said, paused and continued.

"I want you to know I said all that I said because you made me understand I am part of your flesh. Thus, I felt that if you fall; I have also fallen. If you fail, I have also failed. Whenever any negative thing happens to you, I will be the first person to suffer it. I spoke because I felt your success is my success. I thought I could help you see things the other way so that you can assess things better. However, now, I have just realized that you think differently. I am very sorry for being such a source of discouragement to your faith walk. I will go to my father's house and ensure that I no longer be a discouragement to your work of faith. However, I want you to know that I love you. I love you so much. I did all I did because I love you. I wish you the best," Juliet said in the midst of her tears.

She wiped her tears and tried to hold it back but it continued to flow down freely. She allowed the tears to flow freely as she walked out of the room. She couldn't hold back the tears that were flowing down her cheek. The tears flowed down to express the pain of her heartbreak. As she walked out, Ebitobho felt a strange emptiness within him but he tried to control his emotions.

Other times, when they had any disagreements, he ensured that they settled the matter before she left his house. However, on this occasion, he allowed her to walk away without making any attempt of calling her back to fix things up with her. Juliet gently closed the door behind as she walked out of the room and left.

Chapter 12

The sudden breakup of the two lovers continued to torment Ebitobho right from the very moment Juliet left the house. He was so restless and depressed. The thought of not seeing her for a long period of time weighed him down. He laid straight on his back on the bed for a while and then he stood up. He walked round the space in the room for a while, then he went to the chair and sat down. He sat down on the chair for a while and then he stood up and began to walk round the space within the room again.

Several thoughts continued to battle for dominance in his heart as he walked around the space in the room. It was a ceaseless clash of opinions as he tried to condemn and justify his decision and action. He had never had such emotional distress in the past. All the times he had put an end to a relationship years ago; he never felt anything. However, this one seemed to give him a lot of concern. He was troubled about so many things he had not thought about before the breakup. The ease at wish he used to do such a thing in the past and was not perturbed about it seemed to have eluded him. He battled with the thoughts which continued to invade his mind.

"How could you do such a thing to her when she just returned from a long journey? You did not even allow her to have some rest. That was very cruel," a voice blamed him.

"But she caused it. She was so impatient. I told her to be patient but she wouldn't listen. She brought it upon herself so let her bear it," Ebitobho countered.

"You did not handle the situation properly like a man. Don't you think every woman would be impatient when they face such a shocking situation? You never gave her any hint. She just came and met an empty house that was fully furnished when she left for school. You didn't do well. You should apologize and seek for forgiveness," the voice blamed him again.

"Well, I handled the situation the best way I could at the moment. Now, I can't change the hands of time. I have already made my decision and voiced it. There is no going back. We have to face it. She is not the only one suffering it. I am also suffering it here," Ebitobho countered.

"Don't you think this is hypocritical? Your heart still yearns for her and you know. How could you allow such a misunderstanding to tear you apart? Are you sure you have done the right thing? After all, she was just trying to advise you and she has the right to do so. You have shown her your intention of making her your wife. When she feels you are not taking the right decision, she ought to talk about it because she will also suffer it if she keeps quiet," the voice said.

"But this relationship is making me commit the sin of immorality and that is against the doctrines of my faith. This will keep us apart for a while," Ebitobho replied.

“If that is what you want to prevent, is it not better to tell her plainly than for you to use a different thing as a criterion to push her away? As it stands now, she does not even know that is one of the reasons you are pushing her away. If you tell her, maybe, both of you could think and devise a better means of handling the issue than for you to break up with her in this manner. You took the wrong approach. You should apologize and reconcile with her.”

“But she is becoming a source of discouragement to me. Her perception on this subject is very contrary to mine. If we stay together, we will continually argue and quarrel about such issues. I am not ready for such clash of opinions.”

“She only wants the best for both of you that was why she gave her sincere opinion. You need to look at it from her viewpoint too and assess the subject again. No one knows it all. We learn every day, even from children.”

“I don’t need her viewpoint on this matter for now. She will not agree with me on this subject. Her words have expressed her mindset. I am sure that her course of study will always give her a good stand to argue with me and discourage me on this subject. Faith is always rooted in the wisdom of God. Human wisdom is from the senses. The both kinds of wisdom will always be in disagreement and I am not ready for that now. When my actions have provided credible proofs, then we can talk about it. Right now, I am not ready to face her constant opposition on this matter,” he replied.

That response seemed to have silenced the blaming voice of his mind, nevertheless, after a while; the voice came up with more questions to discredit his decision and action.

"Don't you think if you give her some books and tapes, it will make her see things the way you do?" the voice countered again.

"What if I give her the books and tapes but it doesn't still make her change her perception on the subject? I think I have done the right thing for the moment. I have no regret about what I have done. I don't like anybody to come between me and my beliefs and my services to God. My faith is the most important thing to me right now," Ebitobho said to himself.

"Are you sure you still want her as a wife?" the voice asked.

"Yes, of course. I still want her as my wife. However, we are not ready to settle down for now. So we can remain like this until we are ready to settle down."

"If she gets hooked up to someone else during this period that both of you are not together; what will you do?" the inner voice asked him again.

That question stirred up so much fear and worry in his heart. The thought of losing her to someone else troubled him. He became very restless. He began to walk round the space in the room. Then, suddenly, he heard a knock at the door and he was startled. He wondered if Juliet had returned to sort things out with him. He breathed heavily to calm the tension that was building up within him. He turned and faced the door, took a step forward but stopped abruptly. He breathed heavily again as the knock came louder the second and the third time.

"Hold on! I will get it," Ebitobho replied as he walked to the door and opened it.

It was his friend, Ifiyemi. Immediately he saw his friend, the tension in his heart immediately disappeared.

"Good evening my dear. Please, come in," Ebitobho said.

"Good evening," Ifiyemi said as both of them took their seats on the upholstery chairs.

"How has your day been?"

"It's been fine. Thanks."

"And how has yours been?" Ifiyemi asked, looking at him very closely.

"It has been fine too," Ebitobho replied.

"Your looks suggest something different. You look so terrible! What is happening to you?"

"I am fine," Ebitobho replied.

"You are not fine. I can see it clearly on your face. What's eating you up gradually like a virus?"

"I don't understand what you are saying."

"Stop acting as though you don't know what I am talking about," Ifiyemi replied with a cold tune. "I met Juliet walking out of your house in tears. I took her to my house and found out that you asked her to go home. You told her you wanted a break, and that she should stop coming to your house because she is becoming a source of discouragement to your walk of faith."

"Yes, I did. She was condemning, castigating and mocking me for giving my electrical appliances as a seed offering. Is she the one who bought them for me? Is she the one who gave me the job? Is she the one who gave me life? How dare she challenge and ridicule me for my decision? I want us to take a break. I want to be alone for now. I want to be free to serve my God the way I want. I don't want unnecessary interrogations, arguments and discouragement about my decisions and actions when it comes to my service to God," Ebitobho said with a tone of seriousness.

Ifiyemi remained quiet for a while. He does not want to say anything that will worsen Ebitobho's bad mood. After remaining silent for a while, Ifiyemi called the name of his friend to break the silence.

"Ebitobho!"

"Yes, I'm here."

"I decided to keep quiet about this issue when I discovered you couldn't speak boldly on the subject to convince me when I asked you the day you were taking your things to church. I was indeed shocked to my bones when I saw what you were doing. I know that you started this before I joined a church that's why when you did what you did, I decided to remain silent hoping that someday you will make me understand the 'revelations' behind your actions. If I was also attending your church, then I would have had some insights to your 'revelations' and motivations. However, I must confess to you today that I am still nursing my complete astonishment over your action. If I could still be so astonished by your actions, then I wonder how Juliet might have felt today when you told her what you did," Ifiyemi said, paused for a while and continued.

"I know you are a very zealous person and that could make you take certain decisions about what you believe sometimes, however, when you want to take decisions that will affect other people, especially people who are part of your life, you must always learn to consider their opinions on the matter. You cannot always take decisions without coming to agreement with them. For instance, concerning this particular situation, you should have told her and agreed with her before going ahead to do so. Juliet is not just your friend, she is your fiancée. You have already shown her to your mum and she has already accepted the young woman. It is no longer a secret affair even though her parents are not yet aware of it. Sadly, she was not even here when the decision and action was taken. So all her interrogations, criticisms and possible ridicule could have only been directed to correct such reoccurrence in the future."

"I don't want any correction, interrogation, and criticism" Ebitobho interrupted. "I have made up my mind to even give more until I prove the subject of giving. I will continually give my best and my all until I prove it. That's why I don't need her around for now. I can only bring her around when my convictions have been proved and I am ready to settle down with her."

"No one is an island of wisdom. Wisdom has nothing to do with age. Every human being is endowed with some kind of wisdom in a specific aspect of life. Some could be on spiritual matters, while some on financial matters. Some could be on home management, while some could be on job or business management. And even though, sometimes, two people could be gifted on the same aspect of life, their perceptions, explanations and applications could be quite different," Ifiyemi said and paused again for a while before he continued.

"Every religious belief is a very sensitive subject matter. It demands some extra caution. I have heard brothers kill their own brothers because of some religious belief. I have also heard parents kill their own children because of some religious belief. Most of the wars, crisis and terrorism in the world today are stirred up by some religious belief. I have noticed that religious belief is the only thing that can corrupt the power of love a man has for his fellow human being. And when a man becomes too fanatic about his religious beliefs; he becomes a misfit to the entire human society."

"Please, go straight to the point. You are dancing around too many issues," Ebitobho interrupted.

"I am sorry for dancing around so many issues. However, please, I want you to be patient. Give me your ears for today. I will not talk about this matter another day. Please, let me take my time and pour out everything that has been in my mind all these days that I have been quiet," Ifiyemi pleaded.

"Alright, go ahead," Ebitobho said.

"I think the message of giving has become a subject that is continually abused by many preachers, and also misunderstood by many believers. The truth remains that it is more blessed to give than to receive. However, we should endeavour not to allow ourselves to be so enthusiastically carried away by the wind of every doctrine on the subject, to the extent we find ourselves shift away from the norm into some fanatic excesses and extremities. We must always endeavour to strike a balance. In as much as we will give and will always give; the 'dangerous giving' perception that will make us do the kind of things you did should be done with caution so that we will not continually have clash of belief with our loved ones. Remember, they are the ones that will suffer from our decisions and actions," Ifiyemi said, then he paused and continued.

"I know that I have not read through the whole Bible. However, from the little I have heard and read, occurrences where people gave their best or everything they had, sacrificially, did not happen continually. They only did it once or twice. King Solomon who offered thousands of burnt offerings gave from the abundance of the wealth he inherited from his father, David. I have not read any portion of the Bible that says King Solomon did that continually all his life. If you study that account, you will notice that no one cajoled him to do it. Meaning, he might have done it from his heart as an act of worship to God. He did not do it with an expectation of getting God make him wealthier. If you study the Bible, you may notice that those who gave their 'all' either did it because they heard directly from the mouth of a prophet or they did it generously. You will notice that when they gave, there were instant results. They did not give that way habitually all their life. They did it once or twice as an act of worship. They did it in a state of hopeless. Before I continue, let me ask you this question but please, keep the answer. Before you parked your things to sow as seed faith offering, where you in any hopeless financial situation? Do you think the pastor you gave those things really needed those things? I know that when Elijah demanded that the widow of Zarephath should give him the meal first, he was really hungry. Elijah needed the food that was why I guess an instant miracle took place when she obeyed. They ate from that same pot until the famine was over. Sometimes, in the bid to encourage people to give, I think some preachers erroneously use the enticing words of human wisdom to persuade their congregation to give. There is no doubt in my heart that God will surely reward their labour of love. However, we have to be cautious. I am not against the message of giving. I also give in church. I am not against you giving to men of God too. Nevertheless, I would have preferred if your giving will meet a peculiar and relevant need in their lives just like the widow of Zarephath met the need of feeding Elijah. I know that some of the things I have said may not be perfectly correct however, what I am trying to say is that you should give wisely," Ifiyemi said.

"I have heard you, my friend. Thank you for your advice," Ebitobho said.

"One more thing... I want you to reconsider your decision and action concerning your relationship with Juliet. Both of you have come a very long way. Breaking up in this manner does not sound good to me. If you have really decided to marry her just as you have always told me, then you should respect her opinion. If you ask me, I will tell you she has not done anything wrong to deserve what you have done. She was just performing her duty as your wife-to-be. She is carrying your second pair of eyes. If your own pair of eyes is not seeing properly, you can see properly with her eyes; for that is the essence of every relationship. We are supposed to strengthen each other. When you opened your mouth to say you want to marry her, you gave her the right to function as your wife even though it has not been legalized. The most important thing about every relationship is the decision that both of you took behind the scene to live together. Based on that decision, one of her duties is to advice you when she feels you are doing the wrong thing. It will be very unfair and wrong if you use that as a criterion to break-up with her. She has gone home but I want you to fix things up with her. I will see you later," Ifiyemi concluded and left.

The streams of thoughts that continued to trouble Ebitobho gradually returned as Ifiyemi left his house. The advice he had received from his friend also helped to stir it up again. He stood up from the chair and went to the bed. He sat on the bed and laid straight on his back, his eyes facing the ceiling. Then he rolled from one side of the bed to the other to get some comfort on the bed but he couldn't. He stood up, walked to the door and looked outside.

It was already the cool of the day. Although it was not yet dark, however, night was around the corner. The sun was sinking gradually into the western horizon. The children of his neighbours were playing outside. Then, Ebitobho suddenly decided to take walk around the neighbourhood. He closed the door behind him, locked it and began to stroll out, greeting those who were sitting outside.

Chapter 13

One year later, Ebitobho concluded with his first degree programme at the university. Nevertheless, few days to the day of his convocation ceremony, the oil company he was working with was shut down due to some political problems. Sadly, none of their entitlements were paid. Their local and national unions did all they could to ensure that all their entitilements were paid but it did not yield any result.

Ebitobho started looking for another job. He moved from one company to the other and from one establishment to the other to dropped his curriculum vitae. Days passed and turned into weeks. Weeks passed and turned into months but none of them called him for any interview. He made new copies of his curriculum vitae and went to other companies and establishments but none yielded any immediate result. Soon, things became very difficult for him that he found it very difficult to even eat a good meal some days. He had never thought throughout the thirty days of the month, he could struggle so hard to earn a kobo in his life.

One day, after moving from place to place in search for a job; Ebitobho returned home with an empty stomach and pocket. As he sat on his cushion chair to have some rest, the sharp fangs of hunger pieced his stomach walls mercilessly to remind him that he had not eaten anything since morning. Even the previous night, he went to bed without a good meal.

He yawned noisily and stretched himself. The hungry and angry worms in his stomach grumbled and rumbled alongside the cracking sound of his body. He stood up and walked to the bed. He laid straight on his back and looked at the ceiling. There was no doubt the mid-day sun was doing a fantastic job, setting fire on the roof of the building. The weather was very hot and most houses had turned into ovens for their occupants. Even NEPA had joined hands with the forces with nature as they refused to supply electricity.

The room was very hot but he remained on the bed. He sighed continually to express his frustration as the war in his stomach continued to get more intensed. Suddenly, his mind began to journey into his past. He remembered how things were very rosy for him years ago. He remembered how he had refused all the counsel of his friends, especially Juliet and Ifiyemi concerning some of his decisions. Suddenly, he began to remember some of the words of Juliet.

"Let me tell you something; any man who cannot fall back on another means of income immediately he loses his job is doomed for hardship. I can see it coming but you have been so blinded by your beliefs. I know you will never see it because you have been indoctrinated. I only advised you because there is something I am seeing that you are not seeing. I could be wrong but I pray that you always have more than enough to give. I pray that you will never come to a point in your life where you start looking for help from people. I pray that your faith works for you always. Let it produce the remarkable results you have desired and expected, else you will also learn your lesson like my father in a very hard way."

Ebitobho shook his head and sighed again.

"Why are things getting so tough for me? Did I do the wrong thing for being such a 'dangerous' giver or did I do the right thing in a wrong way?" Ebitobho asked himself as he sat up from the bed suddenly.

He stood up from the bed, walked towards one of the upholstery chair, and sat down. He sighed continually as he used one of his palms to support his jaw. He wondered if God had not seen all his sacrificial giving. He wondered how God could allow him to get to such a level that he could find it so difficult to have a good meal these days.

"Was the Bible lying to have said that give and it shall be given unto you, good measures, pressed down, shaken together and running over shall men give unto your bosom?" he asked himself silently. "Did I misunderstand the Scripture about giving? Why are things happening the way they are? Well, may be; I still have to be patient but.... Oh God! What should I do now? I need to eat," Ebitobho said to himself silently.

"Today is one of the days for counseling in church. Why not go and see your pastor. He might give you some assistance," a voice suggested.

"Great! That is it! I will go and see my pastor and tell him what I am going through," Ebitobho said to himself.

He had not told his pastor about the financial difficulties he was facing due the loss of his job. He picked his bunch of keys and walked out of the room. He locked the door and walked towards the gate of the Marine Estate. He walked to the church office under the scotching heat of the mid-day sun. When he arrived at church, only few people were on the cue, waiting to see the pastor. He waited for a while and it soon came to his turn to see the pastor. He stood up from the white plastic chair he had been sitting on and walked to the chair that had provided for him in front of the pastor.

"Good afternoon, pastor," he greeted as he took his seat.

"Good afternoon, son of consolation. How are you?"

Ebitobho smiled as his pastor called him son of consolation. That name suggested that his pastor knew something about his sacrificial acts of giving in church.

"I am quite fine, pastor," Ebitobho responded.

"Speak like a man of faith, Bro Ebitobho," the pastor admonished with a smile.

"I am fine," Ebitobho corrected himself and gave out a dry smile which faded out almost immediately.

"Better! Let us pray," the pastor said and they had a short prayer. "Now, tell me your challenges," the pastor said after the prayer.

"Pastor, I have lost my job and things have been so difficult for me. I could hardly eat a good meal these days."

"That is a minor problem. You have been such a son of consolation in this church. However, I noticed that you have not been giving big for some time now."

"Yes, I know. I have not been giving as I used to give because I have lost my job. Even our entitlements have not been paid," Ebitobho replied.

"I see. Be of good cheer! Your time of change has come."

"Amen," Ebitobho echoed excitedly.

"I want you to know that it is during such periods of hardship that you experience the power of God. Before any challenge comes to a Christian, God has already given him the solution. I will pray for you but the fastest way to change your present circumstance is for you to take a 'dangerous' seed faith offering to the altar. You have been taught this truth and you know what to do. Ensure that you direct the seed offering to the anointing in the life of your man of God and the Lord shall indisputable supply all your needs according to his riches in glory," the pastor said.

"But pastor...."

"Let me pray for you and things will definitely change for the better in your life. Your season of miracle has come," the pastor interrupted.

The pastor held hands with him and prayed for him. After the prayer, the pastor told the usher to call the next person that was waiting. Reluctantly and speechlessly, Ebitobho got up from his chair and walked out of the church premises. He walked home slowly as if his legs were heavy. With his two hands in his pocket and his mind deep in thoughts, he walked slowly as though he was trying to prevent his legs from stepping on some dangerous elements on the ground.

He remembered his several acts of 'dangerous' giving in church in the years past. Ebitobho remembered the last encounter he had with Juliet that brought about their separation. He recalled all the things she said to him on that day. He recalled his discussion with Ifiyemi after his breakup with her. He recalled everything Juliet and Ifiyemi said to him vividly. They all replayed clearly in his mind. He sighed again and again as he continued his walk home. He regretted ever going to meet the pastor. He regretted and blamed himself for closing his ears to all the advice of his friends.

"What have I done to myself? I have made myself a victim. I have made myself a prey to the predator. I can now see that Juliet was right after all. My immaturity and overzealousness landed me in this desert. I have learnt my lessons in a very hard way. The elders are right when they say that the foolish fly that rejects advice follows the corpse into the grave," Ebitobho said to himself silently as he sighed again and continued with his walk in deep thoughts.

"Indeed, the illusion of wealth blinds the eye of the rich and makes him think that lack does not exit but the flood of difficulties washes away that royal blindness. The child that is impulsive, rash and hasty can never appreciate the words of wisdom until Life, herself teaches him. Difficulties is helping me see things better. Oh! How I wish, I had listened to Juliet and Ifiyemi!" he lamented.

Ebitobho recalled one proverb after the other that he had heard from his father and his mother whenever they gave him any piece of advise. The same proverbs that had meant nothing to him were beginning to teach him so much about the realities of life as he walked home slowly under the heat of the sun, engulfed in deep thoughts.

"I don't think I did the wrong thing for giving. It is good but... Em... I think I was just too overzealous about it and I fell into the ditch of extremism because of my ignorance. What have I done to myself? If I had only listened to Juliet and Ifiyemi, I would have reduced the impact a bit. If those who love you cannot correct you, then, who will correct you?" Ebitobho asked himself "*Chai!* I should have listened to them," Ebitobho said to himself as he continued to walk home.

"But wait a minute! So my pastor could allow me to go home in hunger? I can't believe this," Ebitobho said silently to himself as his mind wondered from one thing to another.

"He may not even know the level of hardship you are going through," another thought countered. "Sometimes, people can never know what you are going through even when you tell them. Most times, they still look at you from the viewpoint of where they met you in the past," that thought suggested.

"Yeah! But he did not give me a listening ear. He seems to wave it off tactically by calling for the next person. If he sincerely wanted to help, he would have not just discharged me when it was obvious I still had something to say."

"Do you know if he is tired? Do you know if he does not have any money on him? You can never tell if he is actually rushing to attend to everyone so that he can catch up with another appointment. Remember, he is a man like you and he also has his personal challenges he may be facing at the moment and that may also affect the way he has responded to you today. I think, you should see him again another day," that thought suggested.

"See him another day! I can never go to see him on this matter again. God will help me go through it even though I don't know how

He will do it. Now I have come to realize that my help comes from God alone. I will look up to Him and wait on him to send help from Zion," Ebitobho said to encourage himself.

When he finally arrived at home, it was almost 5.00pm and he went straight to bed with his empty stomach. He laid straight on the bed with his back as he focused his gaze on the white ceiling. He waited for sleep but it refused to come to his aid. He just wanted to sleep and forget the present predicament but he couldn't sleep off. His problems had swallowed the influence of sleep on him. His eyelids refused to yield to sleep. His busy mind kept wandering from one problem to the other.

"I don't blame those who do all kinds of despicable things to put food on their table," Ebitobho said to himself. "How can any one allow such a fierce battle to take place in one's stomach and wouldn't take any drastic step to do something to calm it? This hunger can indeed drive someone to do the incredible and the unbelievable. Gosh! I have never been so hungry in my life."

"I don't think this kind of hunger is new to you. You have fasted for more than thirty-six hours in the past without food. This is not even up to a good twenty-four hours," that thought reminded him.

"Yeah, but that is a different scenario. I was feeding very well before I began the fast. When I was fasting during those periods, I was not in such a hopeless state, where I could not tell when my next meal will be in front of me; and that makes it worse. Gosh! Life could be very funny sometimes. I won't have believed if someone told me I will experience what I am going through right now," Ebitobho said to himself.

Ebitobho was awakened from his long slumber to the sweet and bitter realities of life. That was the first day in his life he had to go to bed with an empty stomach because he had no money to feed himself. All his life, he had never known lack let alone having nothing to eat. He started struggling to earn money from a very tender age. Even though he was the thirteenth child to a polygamous family of four wives and fourteen children, where his mother was his father's last wife; he never knew hunger.

Although, he started struggling to fend for himself at a very tender age, however, it was not because of hunger. It was just for clothing. His mother had only two children, himself and his younger sister, Pere. They were the youngest children of their father, Kemelayifa, who married their mother at an old age. Although, their father was still quite strong, however, he could no longer provide enough for the large family and all the wives and their children had to start fend for themselves when he was a about fifteen.

Ebitobho came to the city immediately he finished his secondary school education with the intention to do some casual jobs in order to continue his education. Fortunately for him, when his uncle brought him to the city, the man secured a casual job for him through a friend in an oil company. He started working with the company as a casual. His hard work made one of the white men to like him. He had barely worked for one year when favour handpicked him and he became a member of staff, from a cleaner to a junior staff, through the help of the white man.

Ebitobho continued to think about his life. He sighed and shook his head continually. Thoughts and thoughts and thoughts were all he could feed on that night.

"Life can be so cruel sometimes," he thought silently, "but its cruelty trains and builds a man into maturity. If one can learn from one's mistakes; then one can become a better person. If one can stand up after the fall; then one's legs will become firm on the ground. Life uses the good and the bad to train and build us. How can you stand firm if you don't fall very hard on the ground? A great fall is good if you can learn from your mistake. Only a fool falls, but refuses to learn anything from his fall. Rather, he ends up blaming the people around him. I will not blame anyone for my predicament. It's a great lesson of life for the future," Ebitobho said silently to himself as he continued analyzed his mistakes and his current situation.

"I think my greed has also contributed to my present financial condition. I was never satisfied with what I have rather I wanted to make God to do more. I never acknowledged that eating three square meals every day was indeed a great blessing from God. I wanted more. I was looking for more. I allowed greed to becloud my reasoning. I wanted to force God to do some magic instead of utilizing the resources that he had given to me just like Juliet said. I was too desperate for more."

"Are you saying that it is wrong to desire and aspire for greater things in life?" another thought countered.

"Hmm... Desiring and aspiring for greater things is not wrong. However, one must acknowledge the stages of growth. When a nine years old child begins to desire and aspire to drive a car at his tender age; then such a desire must be checked else, the child will destroy himself. I think, that is similar to my situation. I wanted to grow suddenly into a millionaire through my giving. I wanted to force God to do something remarkable through my giving. I never knew that whatever I possess was a gift and a blessing from God."

"Don't you think your own case is different? You didn't give to force God to do something. You were stirred up by the Word of God. So you did not do anything wrong. Since you acted on the Word of God, you have to remain on the Word of God and allow it produce the results you were expecting. Who can lift a man that God has not lifted? Who can bring down a man that God has lifted? Every good and perfect gift comes from above, from God Himself; not from any human. You should not be looking up to men for help. God is your only present help in the time of need. He is the only One who promises never to leave us. You have to encourage yourself in the Lord like David. Hold on to your faith. Let your current experience strengthen your faith in the God that you have always trusted. You will surely reap if you don't faint. This circumstance is subject to change. Who gave you the job that you lost? If He was the one who gave you the job, then he will give you another job. He is the One who gives his people the power to get wealth. He takes pleasure in the prosperity of His servants. Hold on! Don't give up! Your miracle is on the way and this present challenge will end in praise," the thought enlightened him.

"Hallelujah!" Ebitobho suddenly exclaimed. "Yes! Yes, that is it. It can only get better. I am not moved by what I see. I am not moved by my present circumstance. I am only moved by the Word of God. The Word of God will produce results in my life. I will not give up. He is my source. Christ in me, the hope of glory. Greater is He that is in me than he that is in the world. It can only get better. For the path of the just is like a shining light that shines brighter and brighter unto the perfect day. When the righteous falls seven times, he will surely rise up again; for the Lord is my Helper, a present help in time of need. I am not moved by what I see. All things are working together for my good. Things are getting better. I am making progress. God loves me. Therefore, I will continually trust in him," Ebitobho said to encourage himself.

The atmosphere of hope suddenly enveloped him as he began to encourage himself. Though he was hungry, he seemed to experience some inner peace, strength and joy. He allowed himself to enjoy the euphoria of his suddenly excitement about life. Then, after a while another stream of thoughts began to flow again.

"I broke off with everyone who tends to talk some sense into my head. Oh God! How can I reconcile with Juliet? It will be easier to reconcile with Ifiyemi, whom I told to get out of my house and never come back when he came again to advise me about the way I was still giving 'dangerously'," Ebitobho contemplated.

"Oh God! I would really like to reconcile with Juliet but what will I tell her? How can I face her after all these years? She is the only one that I have loved but I let her go. Will she ever forgive me? Even if she does, can she still give me a place in her heart when I have brutally and heartlessly stabbed her with my words in my ignorance? Oh no! She was supposed to be my wife and she ought to participate in such sensitive decisions but I ignored her. Instead of trying to think reasonably with her; I told her to take a break. Worse still, I turned down all her attempts to reconcile with me. Oh God! I wish I could turn back the hands of time. What will I tell my mother? She told me she does not want to see another woman with me apart from Juliet," Ebitobho contemplated.

"Well, the mistake has been made. It is time to fix the mess and move on. Any problem that could not kill you would definitely make you strong. I will apologize to her but if she does not give me a place in her heart again, I will move on. As for Ifiemi, I know we can sort things out more easily. The past is gone. The mistakes have been made. It's time to correct the mistakes and move on. It can only get better. Yes, it can only get better!" Ebitobho said to himself.

He dropped from the bed, knelt down beside his bed, and spent some time to pray and ask God to help him. After, spending some time to pray, he climbed the bed and tried to get some sleep but it was not deep enough because of the empty stomach. He was alert to every noise in the neighbourhood. Whenever, he woke up, he continued with his prayer on the bed. He prayed until he slept off. Any time he woke up, he continued with his prayer. That was how Ebitobho spent that night.

Chapter 14

Ebitobho had been trying to reach Juliet but his effort had not been productive. From the information he had gathered from one of her friends, Juliet was in school. He had been waiting patiently for her return since then. However, from the same source, he heard that she was in Port Harcourt to spend the Christmas Holiday. Thus, he decided to visit her surprisingly.

Ebitobho left the house when darkness was already covering the land. The roads were very busy. Most of the vehicles in the city were on the road at this period. People were either returning home from work or from their business engagement or the other. He walked down to Lagos Bus-stop and took a cab that was heading to Rumuola.

He was the second person that joined the cab at the bus stop. However, immediately he sat comfortably in the taxi, other passengers filled the remaining spaces. The driver ignited the engine of the vehicle and they drove off. The driver inserted a CD and the first song that the car stereo began to play was "Sweet Memories" by Whitney Houston. The next song was "I Still Believe" by Mariah Carey. The third song was "Always Be My Baby" by Mariah Carey. "The fourth song was "Save The Best For Last" by Vanessa Williams.

These songs caught Ebitobho's attention as they played one after the other. These were some of the songs he had enjoyed with Juliet when they spent time together. Mariah Carey and Whitney Houston were Juliet's favourite female music artistes when they were dating. Ebitobho relaxed and enjoyed the songs one after the other as they continued their journey. No one dropped until they all got to Rumuola, so it was quite a fast drive.

Ebitobho paid for his fare and dropped from the cab. Her resident was not far from Rumuola Junction. So he decided to walk down to her place when he dropped from the car. It was already dark when he arrived at her place. He knocked at the door and she opened the door. She winked her eyes in surprise. Luckily for him she was the only person at home. Her parents and her younger sister had gone to church. Her two elder brothers were not at home too.

"Hey!" she exclaimed. "Who am I seeing? Am I dreaming or seeing a ghost?"

"You are not dreaming. You are seeing a ghost with flesh and blood. Fear not! This one does not disappear like the other ghosts you have seen," he responded with a smile.

"Who told you that I have seen a ghost before?"

"I heard it on Nigerian Television Authority," Ebitobho replied, still smiling.

"Hmm! I see. Was it from Tales by Moonlight or Story Land?" she asked.

"All of the above," Ebitobho replied with a chuckle.

“Please, leave all those tales and come inside,’ she said, paving way for him.

“Thank you,” Ebitobho said.

He walked into the sitting room and allowed his eyes to travel from one end of the room to the other. This was the third time he was entering this house. Juliet never allowed him to visit her when they were still dating. The two occasions he had visited her in the past, he had also visited without informing her. He met her parents on the two occasions and she warned him never to visit again. Since then, she was the only one who visited him at his place.

The sitting room was a very large one. There was a brown rug carpet on the floor; four upholstery chairs: a three-seater sofa, a two-seater sofa, and two one-seater sofas; a 21 inches television placed in a large wooden stand; a VHS video player, audio set and other electrical appliances that were also kept in the wooden television stand. The wooden television stand also served as bookshelf. There were several shelves but they were all filled with books. There was no doubt the books were owned by her parents, who were teachers.

“You are welcome. Please, sit down,” she said, offering him one of the one-seater sofas.

“Thanks,” Ebitobho said.

He sat down and rested his back on the chair.

“What can I offer you?”

“A very cold glass of water will just be perfect,” he responded.

She disappeared through a door and soon come back with a white rubber jug of water and a glass cup. She gave him the glass and poured some water for him. He gulped down the content and stretched out the glass cup for more.

"Were you feeling so thirsty?"

"You will soon find out," Ebitobho said.

She filled it again and he gulped it down just like he had done earlier. He stretched out the cup for more. She filled it again and he gulped it down, just the way he had done earlier. He stretched out the glass cup for the fourth time.

"Please, don't kill yourself here with water. I don't have tears to cry for you," she said as she filled the cup for the fourth time.

"If you don't have tears in your eyes socket, just pour water on your head and cry," he said and they laughed.

He did not drink the fourth one as he had been doing. He dropped the cup on a wooden stool beside him and she also dropped the rubber jug beside the cup. She took a seat in the two-seater sofa opposite him. They sat quietly for a while, their eyes fixed on the television.

"How have you been all these years?" she asked finally.

"I am fine but I have been missing you so much lately," he responded.

"I see. So you mean you have not been missing me all these years?"

"That's not what I am trying to say. I am just talking about how much I have been missing you recently."

"It's still the same thing. You said that you have been missing me recently. The missing just started recently. I am not moved by how much you are missing me recently. The truth is that you just started missing me recently. I feel so bad knowing about it because I know how much I missed you from the day you pushed me out of your life. You should have kept it to yourself," Juliet said.

"Please, pardon my use of language. I am very sorry. I have realized my mistakes and I have been regretting my actions. I came here to apologize and ask for your forgiveness."

"I never knew it will take you such a long time to realize your mistakes," she said shaking head. "Well, this is not the right place for us to discuss such an issue."

"Where do you want us to go and discourse this issue?"

"We can go to anywhere but not here."

"Please, choose the place that will be convenient for you."

"Are you still staying at that same place?"

"Yes."

"When can I meet you at home?"

"I will be at home all day tomorrow. So you can come to the house any time of the day."

"Alright. I will be coming to your house tomorrow morning, around 10.00am," she said.

"That will be fine. Thank you," he responded.

"You are welcome."

They changed the subject and discussed generally about school and their families. When Ebitobho was ready to go, he finished the fourth cup of water and informed her about his departure. Juliet saw him off to the road before he finally left her and went home.

Chapter 15

Juliet arrived at Ebitobho's place before 10.00am the following day. The door was open but the curtain restrained her from seeing him inside the room. She walked to the door and knocked gently. He answered from inside and told her to come in. She walked in and looked around with a look of surprise on her face. The room was still as it was when she last visited before their separation.

She sat down quietly and ignored his eyes. Both of them remained silent. None of them could break the silence. It was like a great thick wall seemed to separate them. They sat on their different upholstery chairs opposite each other and remained silent for a long time before Ebitobho finally picked up courage to break the silence.

"Thank you so much for coming to my place today just as you promised yesterday," Ebitobho began.

"You are welcome," Juliet replied with cold tone without looking at his face.

"I want to begin by saying that I am very sorry for all the pain I made you go through. It has not been easy for me either but I had to endure to the point where I learnt my lessons the hard way. I wish I could turn back the hands of time. I wish you could find a place in your heart to forgive me. I am very sorry. Please, forgive me."

"I forgave you long ago. I have not been holding anything against you. I felt; such is life. One has to take it the way it comes and move on," she replied without still looking at his face.

"I have seen what life has offered and I have come to my conclusion that you were right. I was too proud, foolish and naïve to see things from your viewpoint when you were trying to correct me. You were right and I was wrong yet, I victimized you and sacrificed our beautiful relationship for my personal ego and self-righteousness. I have realized that I sacrificed our relationship because of my childishness and foolishness. Now, my eyes have been opened by the realities of life. You warned me but I did not listen. Now, I have learnt my lessons in a very hard way. I want to sincerely apologize to you for the way I treated you. I am very sorry for what I made you go through."

"Did you make me go through anything?" Juliet asked looking at his face for the first time. "You did not make me go through anything. When I met you, I was so naïve about the ways of love and life but now I have gained some knowledge and wisdom. When I first met you, I was a woman but you taught me how to be a man. When I met you, I was weak and you taught me how to be strong and I have learnt to be strong. When I met you, my emotions control me and you taught me how to control my emotions and I have learnt how to control my emotions. When I met you, I trusted you but you taught me not to trust any man and I have learnt never to trust any man. When you told me you wanted a break, you taught me how to be brave. When you made me leave your house crying like a baby, you taught me never to cry because of any man. When I met you, I loved you but you taught me not to love; now I wonder if I can ever love again. I gave you my pride; the pride of my womanhood but you took me for a ride. You got what you wanted between my thighs; I thought you wanted my heart. You made great promises to me and broke all of them. Now, you want forgiveness because life has been so unfair to you. I have forgiven you but my heart is cold towards you and towards all men. When I look at our past, I realized it was just a lesson of life to groom me unto maturity. I have no regrets. You did not make me go through anything; you only taught me some good lessons about life. It was indeed a very good lesson that had made me the new woman I have discovered in me. I love the new woman you have made out of me. I am glad that things happened just the way they did. Just as the Bible says, all things work together for good, indeed, it was for my good. I enjoyed the beautiful times we spent together and I have started enjoying the times we have been apart. I have no ill feeling towards you because I have seen everything as a normal experience of life," she retorted and took her eyes away from him.

Her statement sealed Ebitobho's mouth for a while. He sat quietly and looked at her but she did not look at him. She deliberately took her eyes away from him. They sat there for more than ten minutes without talking to each other. However, finally, Ebitobho broke the silence again.

"Well, even if I did not make you go through anything, I feel guilty for the way I treated you the last time you came here and I am sorry. Please, I want you to forgive me."

"I have told you earlier that I have forgiven you long ago. I am not holding anything against you. What happened, only happened so that each of us could learn from it! You have learnt your lessons and I have also learnt mine. "

"I don't think, you learnt the right things," Ebitobho responded.

"What do you know about right or wrong? I got sick continually like a sickler because you threw me out like a piece of garbage. I was in and out of the hospital for several months. I almost failed out of school in my first year because I did things right. Did I do anything wrong for falling in love with you? Did I do anything wrong for advising you to be cautious about the way you give? Well, your reaction told me that I did the wrong thing. My dear, you have no right to tell me that I learnt the wrong things. What I learnt from the way you treated me is none of your business. It's my life and I am the one that will decide if it is right or wrong. After all, I am the one who will bear the consequences, whether they are good or bad. And now, tell me; when did my decisions become your concern?"

"Your decisions became my concern from the very moment I realized that you were right about all you said to me."

"Well, that's now in the past."

"But it is still important to me because you are the only woman I have loved. I still love you and I still want to marry you just as I said years ago."

Juliet smiled and shook her head. "I am sorry. That is an old story that has lost its glory. I hope you know that I am no longer that naïve girl you dumped over two years ago? My dear, a lot of things have changed because of the things that happened to me. There was a time I desperately longed to hear these beautiful lies from you but you neglected all my pleas and now I no longer want to hear them. Stop wasting your time."

"I did all that I did because of my immaturity. I was not yet matured to handle such things. I have learnt from my mistakes and I will make it up to you if you can only give me one more chance. Please, give me a second chance."

"How can I give you a chance when I can no longer believe or trust your words?"

"I don't want you to trust or believe my words. I just want you to give me another chance."

"My dear, things have changed. I have become a different person. Where do you want me to start from?"

"Let's just start afresh from here. Let's throw the past behind us and start all over again," he said.

"One can never throw away the past because one's past influences one's future. Those who forget their past will be doomed to make the same mistakes of their past in the future. Life is too short and too precious for me to make the same mistakes over and over again. My dear, I have moved on with my life and you've got to do the same."

"Please, my queen, give me one more chance. My experiences have taught me so many things about life. I can never take your love and your words for granted. Please, give me a second chance," Ebitobho pleaded.

"Do you think it is as easy as you think?"

"Please, try. I can give you some time to think about it."

"There is nothing to think about. I have already involved myself in another relationship. What do you want me to do when you never wanted me again? I could not have waited for eternity! Just as I have said earlier, I have moved on with my life. You have to do the same."

"If you can remember, I never said I don't want you again. I only said we should take a break."

"But you were not there for me when I needed you. If you had only taken me as a mere friend; it would have helped. But you threw me out into the rain and abandoned me there. Your love for your religious belief was stronger than the love you had for me. How can you say you love God when you don't love your fellow human beings? If you were in love with me, you would have known what it means to miss your loved one for one day, let alone these years. I know what I went through. I know that if you had gone through half of what I went through, you would have reconsidered your action years ago. But you didn't until you learnt your lessons. Meaning, if things had not turned out the way it is now; you might not have realized yourself. Our beautiful relationship meant nothing to you. I was really disappointed to realize that you never loved me the way I loved you. You loved your religious beliefs so much and you never cared if it was hurting the very person you wished to marry. Were you not supposed to love your wife just the way Christ loved the Church and gave himself for the Church? Your love was so fickle it could not stand the test of time. The love you professed to me was not from your heart. I saw it in your actions, which spoke louder than your words."

"How could you say that? You know I loved you and I still do."

"You can tell that story to babies. I am too matured for such childish stories. You never acted it. I was deceived by your words and you actions told me exactly how you felt about me."

"Why are you talking like this? You know I loved you and I still do."

"I used to believe that but I no longer believe it. How could you say you love me, yet you use your own hand to pick a knife and stab me so bad and never cared if I will be hurt? If you really did, you won't even pick the knife let alone hurting me. But you did. And here you are, talking about love! What is love? Love is more than a mere feeling. It is not just about some wild emotions that are inconsistent and ephemeral. Love is a choice. Love is an expression of that firm decision to stand with the person you have chosen, irrespective of the challenges that come your way. Love ought to compel you to sacrifice every other thing in order to sustain, maintain and retain the relationship you have built. Love requires sacrifice. Love should stand the test of time irrespective of the challenges. Your love failed the test of life. I can't entrust my life to such kind of love. Please, leave that childish story of love. Love is for the matured and not for babies."

"I am sure you can clearly remember that I showed you my love the way I knew best before that ugly experience. I never did anything to hurt you all the period we dated except that day the ugly incident occurred. I am not perfect. Nobody is perfect. I am a human. I have my flaws. I guess, my human weakness played out that day."

"Before you carried out that action, you have been nursing it for some time. Out of the abundance of the heart, the mouth speaks. You only did what you have made up your mind to do and when you had the opportunity, you went ahead to do it without a second thought. Well, someone has helped me to gather all the broken pieces of my heart. He has been there for me all these while and I can't just dump him the way you did and run after you. What if you do the same to me again in the nearest future? Even though we have more beautiful memories, I can't just abandon the one who was there for me when you dumped me. My dear, it is too late."

"I can never do that to you again and you know it," Ebitobho replied.

"I don't know anything. I used to think I knew you before you did what you did without any warning. I wouldn't have believed, even if a prophet walked up to me and told me you will do that to me. Stop saying, you know it. What do I know about you? I don't know anything. I don't know you. I can't vouch for you. When trust is lost, it is forever lost. You can never build anything strong on those broken walls of trust."

"I want you to see what happened from the viewpoint that human beings are not perfect."

"Exactly! That's why I cannot trust your words again. You broke all the promises you made to me in less than fifteen minutes and destroyed my love for you. It took me over one year to associate with men. You had all the chance in the world to reconcile with me during that period. I was waiting for you but you never showed up and now; it is too late. I am sorry. We can only be friends, if you care. Nothing serious can ever occur between us, again."

"But I still love you. I want to marry you."

"You never showed that love when I expected you to show it. I must confess that I still have some feelings for you but it does not matter. It is too late. I have given my heart to someone else that has been there for me when you were not there. He has not done anything wrong for me to dump him. You have to look for someone else. You came late. It's too late. I am very sorry."

"Baby, please," Ebitobho pleaded.

"There is nothing I can do about it for now."

"Please, just give me one more chance."

"I am sorry. You came to my house yesterday. You wanted to talk with me at my place. I told you it was not convenient for me to discuss this matter with you under my father's roof. So I promised to come to your place and I have done that. I have heard everything you wanted to tell me. I have also told you my stand. We have taken some quality time to discuss as adults. And now, I want to take my leave and go back to my father's house," she concluded, stood up and picked her bag.

Ebitobho also stood up immediately and held her hand. "Please, you can't leave now," he pleaded.

"I don't want to struggle with you. Please, leave my hand. You are not the one who told me to come here. I am the one who decided to come here to listen to what you want to say. I decided to come to the house you once said I should not come. I could have given you few minutes to say whatever you have to say at my place but I decided to come because you still have that special place in my heart. We have spoken as adults. You have aired your mind and I have also done the same. Thus, I expect you to understand and respect my decision just as I respected yours on that day you pushed me out of your life. I have stayed much more than I planned. I want to go now, please," Juliet said and he gently released his grip on her hand.

"Before I leave, let me give you a piece of advice. You shouldn't be looking for a wife when you have not been able to take good care of yourself. Marriage is not for those who cannot take good care of themselves. Marriage comes with great responsibilities. Look at your financial status and ask yourself if you are ready to cater for the numerous needs of a stubborn woman like me who loves luxury. When I look at your present situation, I can see that you are not yet ready to provide for the numerous needs of a luxurious wife and her children. My dear, if you open your eyes, you will surely realize that women no longer run after love blindly and end up inheriting the wind. Years ago, love was blind. Today, love is no longer blind. Love has developed great eyes that can see the present and the future. Love looks before it leaps. Love falls in love with the good things of life. Years ago, money can't buy love. These days, money can buy love. If you say that money cannot buy love; then, you are still living in the eighteenth and the nineteenth century. This is the twenty-first century. You've have to wake up and live in the real world that we are living today. Things are changing very fast. Love has developed the intellectual reasoning ability of a human personality and she is also changing with the trend of things. My dear, you have to wake up and stop chasing after things you cannot afford. Love is no longer a cheap commodity. Love is very expensive. Believe me, love is very expensive these days. It takes a loaded wallet, pocket and bank account to get the attention of love. When you have what gets the attention of love;

she will chase after you. Remember, sugar don't chase after the ant. The ant knows how to locate sugar without invitation. It doesn't require any announcemet to identify sugar. That is just the way love is these days. We are living in a new era. Wake up and pursue what you can afford. I am very sure you know your class. The person you dumped me for has elevated my class. Now, I know my class. If your class was higher, I would have reconsidered. You had better look for your class of women. I don't belong to that class again. I don't think the way you do. I don't function the way you do. You know what I am talking about. And one more thing, I don't go back to my past. I only move on. Seriously, I only move on," Juliet said.

"Juliet, are you the one talking to me like this?"

"You taught me the same things. I am only doing things the way you taught me. You planted the seed years ago. Now, you are reaping the fruits of the same seed you planted. I can remember the pain you made me go through for loving you wholeheartedly. You destroyed my love life. You brought pain into my love life and I will never go back to that past. I made up my mind to move on and I have moved on. I will not go back to the pain of my past. Go and look for a girl that belongs to your class! I don't belong to your wretched poverty stricken class," Juliet said with a mischievous smile before she walked out of the room.

Ebitobho sat down on his chair abruptly as if someone had pushed him forcefully to the chair. He could not even think of walking her off to the gate. He remained on his seat and allowed himself to ponder on her words. The words that had proceeded from her mouth had hit him so hard like fiery bullets. Some of her words entered his ears like sharp arrows. Some of her fiery words pieced deep into his head and scattered his brains. Some struck his chest like thunderbolts and ruptured his heart.

He had not expected that her visit would leave him shattered, battered and devastated. He had been expecting a beautiful reconciliation that will mend his past when she promised to come to his house the previous day. However, the realities of her visit have brought him to a new realization that they will never have a future together again. The devastating reality made him feel so bad. Moreover, her last demeaning words were just the bomb. He smiled sheepishly and shook his head.

Chapter 16

It was evening but the weather was still hot. Ebitobho could no longer endure the heat in his room so he decided to sit outside on his neighbour's plastic chair. The roof of the building opposite his apartment had created a nice shade for him outside. That was the building his bosom friend, Ifiyemi, used to live years ago before he packed to another estate within the city. When Ifiyemi was still staying in that building, they usually sat under this shade during this period of the day to chat several times.

Today, as he sat there alone, thoughts about his friend invaded his mind. He allowed himself to think about the beautiful past they spent together within the Marine Estate. As he was still thinking about him, he suddenly raised his face and saw his friend walking towards him. Ifiyemi smiled when he noticed that Ebitobho had seen him and Ebitobho also smiled back at his friend. He immediately stood up from his chair, went and brought another plastic chair for his friend.

"Who sent you to go and get a chair for me? Did I tell you I need a chair?" Ifiyemi asked, still smiling as he walked towards his friend.

“When a friend, whom you have labelled as an enemy, boldly comes to your house without your invitation after you have told him never to visit you again, that friend deserves a chair for his courage. Even if he chooses not to sit down, nevertheless, he still deserves that simple welcoming gesture,” Ebitobho replied, still smiling.

“You never lack words to respond to people at every point in time,” Ifiyemi said, smiling and shaking his head.

“I leant it from you.”

“Both of us know that you didn’t learnt it from me,” Ifiyemi said, still smiling.

“Seeing you today, I wish to say this. There are some people no one can ever fill their places in our hearts. Such people should be allowed to fill those special places in our hearts irrespective of the misunderstanding we may have with them sometimes. I was thinking about you when you showed up. I am so glad that you came. I feel so good seeing you today,” Ebitobho said.

‘Hmm... Beautiful and soothing words of an old friend to a lost friend...Same here, my friend,” Ifiyemi said as they shook hands and hugged each other.

“I am very sorry for the way I treated you in the past. I was wrong, very wrong. Please, forgive me,” Ebitobho said.

“Apology, sincerely and happily accepted,” Ifiyemi said, smiling as both of them hugged each other again and sat down.

“I have been actually longing to come and see you so that I can apologize to you,” Ebitobho began.

“I hold nothing against you, my friend. I forgave you that very day. Being friends does not guarantee that we will not have disagreements. However, we must be matured enough to realize that the ability to handle those disagreements is what keeps people as friends continually."

"Hmm... But you have not visited since you left."

"Well, I just felt I should give you some time. I thought that both of us needed to learn some new things about life before reuniting. Moreover, I wanted to take enough time find out more about what led to our misunderstanding."

"I hope you found out some things."

"You know, it has been said that time is a great teacher."

"Indeed, time is a great teacher and I have been learning a lot these days. But, let's leave that for now."

"Ok. But frankly, I have also been planning to come and see you. I made some stunning discoveries and I felt I should come and share them with you."

"Really? What is it about?"

"Before I begin, I want to appeal to you. Don't look at these subjects with any attachment. I once read that, 'one should never take side with anyone but the Truth. As Christians, we are meant to be defenders of the Truth, which is the Gospel. We are not called to defend persons, positions, or organizations. Our loyalty should always be to the Truth. Some of the problems we have within the Christian community is as a result of blind loyalty. Many Christians commit themselves to a person, position, or an organization, instead of being committed to the Truth of His Word. The problem with being committed to a person is that people are fallible; we make mistakes. Even great Christians can fail, and do things that are very wrong. If you are committed to a person instead of the truth, there is a possibility that you may end up defending the person's actions. This can lead to serious problems of opposition sometimes. The opposition can produce an "us against them" mentality, which often results in divisions.' Please, try and be neutral. Believe me, you will learn something new."

"No problem. But before you begin, what can I offer you?" Ebitobho asked.

"Don't worry. I am fine. Least I forget. How have you been and how have you been faring?"

"Well, it has been very challenging. I have not yet secured a job. I know that though weeping may last for the night but joy will surely come in the morning. Please, let us not go into my recent sad experiences to dampen our happy moods. We can talk about that later," Ebitobho said.

"Alright, that's fine."

"Now, tell me. What are your new discoveries?"

"Em... This may be strange. Although, I still practice them in my church but I discovered from the Bible that tithing, offerings, seed offerings and first fruits are not applicable to the Church."

"Hmm.... This is a very hard nut to crack."

"Indeed, no doubt. However, it is true. You can also study these subjects for yourself. Thank God, we can all possess as many Bible translations we desire. I had to take some time to study the subject of giving when I saw the passionate way you were going about this issue of giving. I felt something was not right about the way you were going about it. So I decided to search the Scriptures for myself and I found out these startling discoveries."

"Alright, tell me about it."

"When you carefully study the style of giving of the early church in the New Testament, you will clearly discover that they gave but they did not give tithes. They gave but they did not give offerings. They gave but they did not give seed offerings. They gave but they did not give first fruit offerings. The kinds of giving most preachers emphasize in the churches these days where not the types of giving recorded for us about the early church."

"This is a very sensitive issue."

"I know my friend. However, I also think there is nothing sensitive about these issues if we can just sincerely embrace the truth written down for us in the Holy Book. Sometimes, I feel that we use some verses of the Scripture to achieve our personal aims. Let me give you an example. When preachers want to preach about tithing, they will only quote verses that support their message. They will never quote or read verses of Scripture which says, *'When thou hast made an end of tithing all the tithes of thine increase the third year, which is the year of tithing, and hast given it unto the Levite, the stranger, the fatherless, and the widow, that they may eat within thy gates, and be filled.'* Preachers will not also tell you that there were people who were exempted from giving tithes. Those whose number of flock or herd were not up to ten never paid tithes. They will not also tell you that Jesus never paid tithes even though he went to the Synagogue several times. However, the same Jesus paid tax and it was recorded for us. Was he in any way valuing the payment of tax more than tithe? Well, I don't know. His disciples who took over from him did not also pay tithes. The disciples did not also tell their followers to give tithes."

"Mehn, I am finding it very hard to swallow these things you are sharing with me today," Ebitobho said.

"Study for yourself. The early church gave big but it was not recorded as tithe, offering, seed offering or first fruit offering. My dear, you have to study it for yourself. Another remarkable and amazing thing in the Old Testament and the New Testament is that the spiritual heads did not manage the things received from the people. They did not dictate what should be done with the things received. In the Old Testament, before they even receive anything, God had already instructed how it should be used. In the New Testament, deacons were selected by the early church to decide how the things received were being used. Sadly, that is not what we see today. I am not saying what we are practicing is wrong, however, I am only saying that was not the practice we find in the Scripture. No wonder, members are always forgotten when they need assistance. No wonder, members get poorer while leaders get richer. In the early church, none among them lacked anything. Apparently, it is no longer a call to service. It is now a call into business to enrich self. So many preachers are now hiding under the umbrella of religion to use gullible minds to actualize their personal gains and goals. I am not saying everyone is doing this. I am not saying you should not give. I am only saying don't allow yourself to fall prey to some of these prosperity teachings. God has already blessed us unconditionally with all things that pertain to life and godliness. The only path to this inexhaustible abundance is your believing. Jesus clearly says in the Scripture that, 'all things are possible to him that believes'," Ifiyemi said.

"Hmm... Amazing!"

"I have not finished. My purpose of coming to your house to discuss this subject with you is not to discourage you from participating in the different kinds of giving in your church; however, you should be able to ascertain when you are shifting towards extremism. I look at the world and I observe that religious beliefs have suddenly turned into a very sharp two-edged sword in the hands of many these days. The shape edges of our new weapon of mass destruction have mutilated and annihilated many around us. We have used it to destroy ourselves and other innocent people. I may not have cared much about it if they use it to destroy themselves alone. However, it has become an issue to me because of the numerous people we hurt every day in the name of some religious beliefs. We have destroyed the lives of many with the same weapon. Our dearly loved ones are usually the first victims of this new weapon of war. Our neighbours and other innocent people immediately join the list when we are done with our loved ones. Sadly, we do not even seem to care about the numerous people who suffer from the brutal swords of our religious beliefs. I have studied a little about some of the major religions on the face of the earth, and I discovered that they all preach peace and love. Sadly, I have also discovered that the most deadly sects on earth have actually emerged from these religious circles. The most deadly people on earth are these religious extremists. I am so amazed that our love for our religious beliefs can even tear apart the amazingly strong bond of love. I weep in my heart when I see great lovers become separated by some religious beliefs. I bleed in my heart when I see parents and their own children become separated by the cruel sword of some religious belief. I am grieved in my heart when I see blood brothers draw swords, and pull guns at each other because of some religious belief. I am saddened when I see loving sisters turned into warring enemies because of some strange religious belief. I mourn for relationships that have been destroyed by the brutal sword of some religious beliefs. My heart is filled with so much sorrow when I see that we love religious beliefs more than human lives and their wellbeing. Believe me, when we commit ourselves to some religious belief more than the way we are committed to our loved ones, it will only end up destroying us. Believe me, when we value some religious belief much more than human lives, and our peaceful coexistence and relationship with other people; then, we will only use it to destroy ourselves. Every true religious teaching should strengthen our bond of love. Every true religious teaching should promote peace in our society. He who destroys others in the name of some religious beliefs has only believed a lie. Soon, he will use it to destroy himself. He may not accept it at the moment; however, if he lives long enough, time will surely make him realize that he has only used it to destroy himself. The world will become a better place if we can only realize that the message of love for fellow humans and the message of peaceful coexistence is the greatest message of all religions. If that is missing, then something is wrong. My dear friend, I will encourage you to go and study the things I have shared with you. Don't believe anything I have said to you. Go and study for yourself and find out the truth for yourself. It is your personal responsibility to find out the truth about what you believe and what you do not believe. It is also your responsibility to know where to strike a balance concerning the things you believe and do not believe so that you can live peacefully with other people in your society, specifically your loved ones," Ifiyemi concluded.

"You have indeed shown that you are a true friend. I will take out quality time to study these subjects you have highlighted. Thank you very much, my friend," Ebitobho said.

The bosom friends spent some time to discuss other issues before Ifiyemi finally left.

Made in United States
Cleveland, OH
20 October 2026

46287531R00097